BOOK 1 OF THE MATCHMAKER SERIES

Mine,
FOREVER & ALWAYS

TAMMY L. BAILEY

Copyright

A Word of Thanks

My Family

My Friends

My Readers

Kathy Sloe for always being willing to read and review my projects.

Heather Belleguelle of Behest Indie Novelist Services.

Chapter One

(London, 1816)

"Please, Lily! You are much more romantic than I am, and so you must write the letter to Mr. Waverley for me! With this, he is sure to know my affections are real, and he will ask my parents for my hand in marriage."

Lily blinked at Jane, both surprised to hear about this Mr. Waverley and amused that Jane Dalton, the most prolific matchmaker of their generation, thought Lily more romantic.

"Otherwise, I will be forced to marry a man who is fifteen years my senior with more hair popping out of his ears and nose than is growing on the top of his round head."

Lily *sighed*, the conversation reminding her of her own unfortunate circumstances regarding marrying well at one and twenty. Although the man her parents had in mind for her was handsome, there was something about his character that set her on edge.

"I'm truly sorry, Jane, but I don't write love letters. I write plays. Besides, how can I pour my heart out to a complete stranger? It wouldn't be genuine."

Her friend scoffed and turned toward the casement window, her bottom lip protruding over her upper lip. Jane's lithe profile was that of a woman who surely had no want of attention. Striking with a fair complexion, cornflower-blue eyes, and soft light-brown curls, she was the envy of every woman between sixteen and sixty. Her appearance contrasted with Lily's forest-green eyes, olive skin, and dark hair. Lily had often wondered whether she would be more memorable if she possessed softer features like Jane's.

"When have I ever asked a favor of you?" Jane sniffed, a handkerchief lifted to her pert nose for dramatic effect.

Lily narrowed her gaze, recalling the day when Jane, bored out of her romantic mind, decided Henry needed to take a wife. Lily, two years younger and infatuated with the heir to Hadley, had agreed to play his young bride in the spirited ceremony.

What she'd thought was a sweet diversion changed her life, and not for the better. Unrehearsed, Henry said his impromptu vows before shifting a peck on the cheek to a firm kiss on her lips. What he uttered next changed her entire world. *Now you're mine, forever and always.*

"Pompous," Lily mumbled. Not only had her "husband" turned out to be an infamous libertine in the seven years since their *wedding*, but he'd also forgotten his words and, along with it, her name, introducing her to one of his lady friends as "Miss Prescott" last summer. Oh, Lily supposed, children had succumbed to sillier pastimes through the centuries. She only wished she'd known to guard her heart before engaging in one of them.

"Please, Lily." Jane rotated around to blink her wispy lashes. "You are my dearest and closest friend. Mr. Waverley must know how I feel. I cannot risk him falling in love with someone else."

Jane's words and her ardent pleading struck a deep chord in Lily's soul. What right did Lily have to deny her friend a chance at happiness? "Very well, but how am I supposed to slip a letter to Mr. Waverley without him believing I was the person who wrote it?"

Jane smiled, her lovely face alight with hope. "I will make sure he is to stay in the guest room across from Henry. We shall wait until tomorrow night after everyone has gone to bed. You will bring the letter to me, where I will sign the bottom. Next, we will sneak to Mr. Waverley's room and slip the note under his door. He will be none the wiser."

Lily hesitated to nod. Always romantic and never sensible, Jane had a way of turning everything into a wedding march of some sort.

"We must, however, keep this letter a secret between us. No one in my family must know, especially Henry. Although he and Mr. Waverley are the closest of friends, my brother would probably shoot him first and ask questions later. He has no tolerance for secrets, you know."

No, Lily didn't. It seemed a lifetime since they'd spent more than a minute in each other's company. A minute where he'd forgotten her name, and she'd forgotten how to speak.

"Now, try not to dally too long. The parlor games will start soon, and I have someone in mind for you." She paused to send Lily a triumphant grin before bending down to give her a kiss on the cheek. "Oh, and if you find yourself unsure of what to write, just imagine a man you love with all your heart."

Jane slipped from the room to give Lily some time to think about what she wanted to write. After many starts and stops, Lily brushed back her thick hair and dipped the quill into the black ink. For once, she wanted to leave her heart out of things. However, with the evening growing late, she resigned herself to take Jane's advice. It might even do her well to confess her feelings and let them go, once and for all.

My Love,

You may have thought of me only once or twice; yet, I have thought of you for what seems all my life. With one slight gaze in your direction, I am lost. I know it seems impossible for me to confess such things, to express an affection that has been unrequited. However, you must know, I have loved you and only you.

At last, Lily laid the quill down, blew out a slow breath, and pushed back in the chair. Although her soul soared with newfound freedom, her mind knew Henry would never see or hear those words from her. They had grown too far apart, creating an invisible wedge between them, so they were little more than strangers.

Discouraged by her thoughts, she swiped at a stray tear and folded the paper, stuffing the confession inside her sleeve. She believed it would remain safer there than anywhere else. Then she plumped up her cheeks and smoothed out her pale-pink empire dress.

Downstairs, the light from two fireplaces and two dozen candles danced about the spacious drawing room and over the six or so well-dressed occupants. She recognized both Mr. Frank Naughton and Mr. Harry Bentley from a previous gathering, as well as the two other women whom Jane had invited and thought suited each gentleman best. Although Lily liked Miss Caroline Putnam and Miss Olivia Carrington, they didn't mingle much, satisfied to remain inside their tight circle of conversation.

"Oh, Lily!" Jane called from somewhere behind her. Both eager and anxious to show her friend the letter, Lily twisted around, stepped, and smacked into a hard and well-proportioned figure. She opened her mouth to apologize when her gaze fell on the victim of her hastiness, Mr. Henry Dalton. Unprepared, her breath left her in a rush, a gesture he noticed and acknowledged with an arrogant lift of one dark eyebrow.

With her heart pounding an erratic beat, she dipped into an awkward curtsey, only to have the letter she had tucked away, fall to her slippered feet. She gasped and reached down to retrieve the love note, a second too late.

"Give that back at once." She straightened as she spoke, her voice lowered to a strained, demanding whisper.

Mr. Dalton lifted the letter to his lips, his gray eyes narrowing over the folded edge. If he smirked or sneered, Lily couldn't tell.

"Am I to assume, Miss…" He paused.

The pompous. "Scott. My name is Miss Lily Scott." She emphasized the last word.

He lowered the letter, his smile wide but void of humor. "Yes, of course. Am I to assume, Miss Scott, that this letter I witnessed fall out of your left sleeve is some intimate diversion meant for someone…in this room?".

Chapter Two

Lily followed Henry's smoky gaze as it shifted from one end of the parlor to the next. She believed he took his time to settle back on her once again. Inside her white gloves, her hands began to sweat. "I wouldn't know, sir."

She answered him honestly. She had never met Mr. Waverley or heard anything about his features. She supposed he was handsome. Jane only liked gentlemen who were, in some way, striking in both character and appearance.

"Now, if you have finished with your questions, I would like to have back what you wrongfully took from me."

Henry slipped the letter into his jacket, smiled, and stepped toward a voluptuous creature with dark, sultry eyes.

Lily dropped her shoulders, recognizing the woman as Henry's latest rumored conquest. At the sight of them together, her stomach churned with nervousness, and her head ached with sudden disappointment. *Oh, God. Why am I here?*

Her thoughts turned to poor Mr. Waverley. Of course, the only thing saving Jane's secret love from a bullet wound was that Lily had neglected to put his name at the top of the letter, and it remained unsigned.

"Did you write the letter?"

Lily jumped and spread her gloved hand over her chest. Her heart thumped against her palm as she rotated around to face her friend. "Yes," she answered, leaving out the fact that it no longer remained in her possession. "It's…written."

Jane clapped her hands like a child. "I'm sure it's perfect, but I'll read it later when Aunt Sophia has fallen asleep," she whispered.

Lily glanced over at the gray-haired woman, her head bobbing one way and then the next, against a red and gold striped mahogany-framed couch. Aunt Sophia remained the preferred relative above everyone else because she always fell asleep during her sole occupation as a chaperone.

"For now, I'm trying to discover what possessed my brother to ask me to invite Miss Appleton," Jane said, all the while smiling in their direction. "They are not together, but I do believe he chooses to associate with the most disagreeable women on purpose, just to vex me."

Lily tried to avoid glancing in Henry's direction by instead sending her friend a sympathetic smile. She'd always remembered Jane as being outspoken and determined. With a much larger dowry than Lily, she attracted her fair share of suitors, all of whom she tried to deflect with her infamous "parlor games." That was until Jane had suddenly and surprisingly realized her unrecoverable love for Mr. Waverley.

"I cannot begin to speculate about Henry's many cordial affairs," Jane continued, fanning her face in disgust. "Do you know that Miss Appleton is rumored to have been engaged five months ago, but the wedding was called off because of something the groom discovered but did not disclose?"

Lily pressed her lips together. While her heart had remained steadfast and loyal to Jane's brother, he'd veered off onto a path of open debauchery. Sometime between their quiet walks in the garden, a lovely pretend wedding day, and this moment, he'd become a man she hardly recognized. What had happened to the young boy who had reached for her hand when he thought her unhappy or hurt? Perhaps she might address him as Mr. Daltrey, next time.

"Oh, good. Look, Henry's unlatched himself from Miss Appleton and is now speaking to Mr. Waverley. I shall introduce you to him."

Lily shook her head. "But I had hoped to have some punch." She needed something to steady her nerves, a place to think on how to retrieve the letter. Since seeing Henry again, her heart hadn't slowed its pace, and her hands had yet to stop shaking. Of course, when she turned away, Jane grasped one of her trembling hands, hauling her toward where Mr. Waverley and Henry stood talking, a glass of brandy in their right hands.

Lily believed she could not imagine Mr. Waverley any more handsome. He was tall with soft blond hair and gentle blue eyes. He was not, however, her *husband*. Stirred by Henry's presence, Lily shifted her gaze to him. Her progress forward faltered when his hand reached into the pocket he'd secured Mr. Waverley's letter. In slow motion, her legs tangled, her ankles twisted, and she landed on the hard floor with a graceless thud.

She lay for a moment mortified and out of breath. The room, already cast in long shadows, drew larger over her. She squeezed her eyes shut, not wanting to comprehend just how miserable she appeared to everyone.

"Are you hurt anywhere?" She flipped her eyelids open to find Henry bent down, his face but a few inches from hers. Unable to yield one coherent word, she shook her head.

"All the same," he said, slipping his hands under her legs and lifting her into his arms.

"This is not necessary," she whispered, hoarse and near tears.

"Put her on the couch, Henry," called Jane's voice behind them.

The letter. "No!"

He halted, his eyes narrowing on Lily's face so long, she thought it might catch on fire.

"I'd...I'd much rather...you take me to my room."

A muscle twitched in his jaw, and she held her breath, waiting to see what he'd do next.

"Very well," he said after a long moment and pulled her snug against him. He carried Lily up the winding staircase, her pulse sputtering with each easy stride.

For propriety's sake, Jane lingered behind them. As he concentrated on his steps, Lily stole glances at his closed expression.

She supposed she'd stared too long at his Grecian features when he cleared his throat, making her jump.

"I don't remember you being this clumsy, Miss Scott," he said, one eyebrow quirking upward.

His mocking and unemotional tone caused the romantic spell he'd woven around her to snap. Drawing in a long breath, she unleashed years of resentment upon his beautiful, arrogant head.

"Since it has taken you this long to recall my name correctly, I'm astonished that you remember anything about me at all."

He exhaled and turned his head, so his lips fell close to touching hers. "I assume you still occupy the same room?" he asked, changing the subject.

His gray eyes turned a shade darker, and she remembered how they'd change when he was running out of patience. "Yes," she said, swallowing hard and loud.

He nodded and rotated sideways to twist the knob to her door. Somewhere between the landing and now, Jane had disappeared.

He grumbled something under his breath, and Lily knew he was not happy with his sister leaving them alone. Still, he brought Lily closer into his sturdy chest. While her mind remained in a state of utmost alarm, her body wanted only to snuggle deeper into his arms. A few years ago, she'd had many whimsical thoughts of this moment, of Henry proposing and carrying her into their new life together. However, like a fool, she'd placed all her hope, all her dreams, on the capricious vow he'd recited to her. She didn't know why he'd chosen to forget her, but it hurt more than anything she'd experienced thus far.

"Are you hurt, Miss Scott?" he asked again, his warm breath laced with a tinge of alcohol.

Yes. "Just my pride, sir," she answered him.

One side of his mouth lifted as he strode across the room, stopping near the side of her canopy bed. He bent to set her down when her arms wrapped tighter around his neck. He couldn't leave her now. She hadn't retrieved the letter.

With her heart in her throat, she pulled Henry's lips to

hers, kissing him as he'd kissed her on their wedding day. The

words he'd said echoing softly in her mind.

Chapter Three

Henry felt Lily's thunderous heartbeat against his chest, felt the naïve tremble in her kiss. He had guessed she'd do something to retrieve the letter from his pocket, he'd just never assumed she'd go this far. He, of course, should have expected it.

More than aroused, he allowed the softness of her mouth to press against his. As she fumbled for the letter, he cupped his palm behind her head, coaxing her closer. Her kiss, sweet like honeysuckle and soft like silk, ignited the blood in his veins. Furious by her attempt to distract him, and yet entranced, he parted her lips with his tongue. She tensed, her fingers halting inside his jacket. Too late to turn back, he stroked the inside of her mouth until he drew a moan from deep in her throat. Her response was a glorious sound, a sound he'd forbidden himself to imagine, until now.

When she'd succeeded in retrieving the item she sought, he pulled away and half-placed, half-plopped her on the bed, grasping her wrist and leaning down toward her reddened, slightly bruised lips.

"The only reason I allowed you to take back the letter is that I've already read it and memorized each word. Although I loathe my sister's parlor games, I have now made it my sole purpose to discover the unfortunate man for whom those words were written."

Her sharp and shallow breaths fanned across his face. "I'm afraid, sir, you will be greatly disappointed at whom you find."

He straightened and left the room. Downstairs, he could not shake what had transpired between himself and Lily. He hated himself for allowing her to kiss him. He hated himself more for allowing himself to enjoy the intimacy between them, if only for that brief moment.

"How is Miss Scott?" Jane asked beside him.

"Slightly…bruised," he answered shortly.

Jane's thin eyebrows rose over her furious blue eyes. "Please tell me you were civil to her."

Henry twisted to face his sister. He knew she remained oblivious to the reasons why he'd chosen to stay away for so many years. Her whimsical illusions regarding love seemed impenetrable, while his had been punctured and left to bleed.

"I am only required to remain civil to those whom I regard as close acquaintances. Miss Scott is a stranger to me, especially since I see her but once every year, and at those times, she can only manage to sputter one-syllable greetings as if my presence offends her."

"She's shy!"

"She's coy, Jane. Women like Miss Scott are not who they appear. I would almost tell you not to see her again."

"You contradict yourself, Henry. First, you say you do not know her, and then you proceed to call her a flirt. Well, which one is it?"

He opened his mouth, only to slam it shut again.

"You could at least get to know her, again."

He lifted his head and inhaled. "I do believe I know her better than anyone else in this room." At least he guessed he did. Of course, he wasn't certain how many other men she'd kissed to get what she wanted.

"Oh, do you claim to know her better than Miss Appleton?" his sister asked, her tone dripping with sarcasm. She sighed loudly before projecting her opinion without pause. "I'm more vexed than offended that you made me invite the woman. It might do you well to stand with someone who hasn't caused a scandal in one way or another."

Amused, he leaned forward so no one else could hear. "And arranging parlor games for young, irrational girls who believe the gentleman whose card they've received will someday want to marry them is not a scandal?"

"Miss Scott is not irrational," his sister hissed, her mouth pursed with irritation.

Henry thought Jane had done a good job of changing the subject back to her friend.

"I beg to differ." He paused, unable to forget how wonderful Lily's soft lips had felt against his. "Regardless, the next time you arrange one of these parlor games and wish to include me, make sure to invite a few ladies who are inclined to converse more than flirt."

Jane scoffed. "Miss Scott is a lovely girl with more intelligence than that…that Miss Appleton you have attached yourself to recently."

Henry wanted to laugh. "I don't like Miss Appleton because of her intelligence."

"Well, that's obvious."

His sister stormed away, going to the writing table to scribble the ladies' names on the cards so the gentlemen could pull them. Not that he admitted to looking, but he found Lily had returned and settled herself on a gold and mauve striped settee next to the window. She had her head bent toward a small book, her teeth biting into the pink flesh of her lower lip. He didn't deny the fact that Lily intrigued him. She had blossomed into such an enticing creature; he could not stop staring at her.

He supposed she sensed him gazing at her and lifted her head to send him a curious glance. She reminded him of their youth and a fleeting time when he thought—

"Pull your card."

Henry bent his head to find Jane standing in front of him, holding a bowl full of shuffled, folded parchment paper.

"Would it do any good to ask which one is Miss Appleton's?"

His sister scrunched up her pert nose and shook her head. Henry wondered how she had not found her own match. Both beautiful and bright, she had her handful of suitors, all of which would have made her a good and proper husband. He imagined she was too romantic to settle for anyone who was not Lord Byron himself.

"If I must say, it would serve you right to pull Miss Scott, Henry."

He had to disagree, for both his and Miss Scott's sake. Nonetheless, he reached in and plucked out a piece of paper. In the glinting firelight, he glanced at the woman's name.

"The devil," he swore. "You have done both her and me a disservice." He left, pivoting toward the awaiting crowd and calling out her name. "Miss Scott."

A few moments later, his friend Waverley picked Miss Appleton's name. Henry had thought he'd feel some jealousy at his friend's great fortune. He did not.

"Now, gentlemen, you are to go to the lady whose name you picked and introduce yourselves," Jane announced with such glee, Henry had to wonder just how much brandy she might have had before the evening began. To his right, Aunt Sophia hiccupped, snorted, and fell back asleep.

As Lily stood reflective and unmoving, he stepped across the maroon carpet, stealing a glance at Waverley, who was, in turn, stealing a glance at Miss Appleton's bosom.

"Mr. Dalton," Lily said, dipping into a curtsey. When she rose, her cheeks were flushed pink, a rather fetching color next to her evergreen eyes. She smiled, causing his heart to beat at a faster pace.

"Sir, if you don't mind me asking, why did you come here, knowing your sister had every intention of luring you into her parlor games?"

He nodded and returned her haughty smile. "I didn't come to be lured, madam, I came to watch."

Her head tilted at an adorable angle. "Are we all so amusing to you?"

Henry exhaled, forced to recall the inviting softness of her lips. "Yes, especially you, Miss Scott. Around the opposite sex, you are the most unsure, unsteady, and undisciplined creature I've ever seen."

Her blush spread lower.

"Do explain, Mr. Dalton."

He stepped a few paces closer, so her chin tilted upward. "A peculiar response. I would have expected you to take offense, lift your hem, and storm off in another direction, perhaps in the company of someone more…complimentary."

He glanced around at the other gentlemen in the room. He'd yet to discover which one she might favor. There was Frank Naughton, who tended to drink more than converse, and Harry Bentley, who, while tall and amiable, did not stand out as anyone who might inspire a lady like Lily to pour out her heart.

When Henry returned his gaze to her face, she blinked her green eyes. "Are you always this crass and unpleasant?" She didn't give him a chance to answer. "And is it your intention to offend me, so I will leave you alone? Are you that desperate to be in the company of Miss Appleton again?"

Henry's heart thumped at her whispered question. Oh, had he heard a tone of jealousy in those barbed words? Although Miss Appleton possessed the type of figure to lure a saint into her bed, he found something about the way Lily gazed at him now that made his blood rush through his veins like a thawing mountain river.

"On the contrary, madam, I don't think I've ever been more engaged in a conversation in all my life. You see, it is not often that I get to converse with a female who has such low opinions of me."

"Forgive me, sir, but I find that hard to believe."

After the initial shock of her forthrightness, Henry threw back his head and laughed. Between the kiss and now, he'd expected her to either languish in remorse or embarrassment. Instead, she talked to him as if they'd never separated.

"Now, it's time to get to know your partner better," Jane called from the middle of the room.

"Oh, dear God," Henry mumbled.

"I don't bite, Mr. Dalton," Lily said beside him.

He turned to her, his chin down, his gaze fixed on her mouth. "It's not your bite, but your tongue I am most…anxious about, Miss Scott."

His bold words caused her to draw in a deep breath. He waited for a response, half expecting her to slap him across the face or, worse, tell him she wished never to see him again. Of course, she continued to surprise him by leaning in, so her words stayed just loud enough for him to hear.

"When you steal something of mine, I will use whatever means to get it back. As well, you should know that it shall never occur again."

He smiled. "Which part: carelessly losing the letter to your lover or kissing me?"

She opened her mouth, only to snap it shut when Jane jumped in with the instructions on what everyone should do next.

"Now, I would like every lady to reach into their partner's jacket and find their handkerchief."

"Oh, dear God." It was Lily's turn to whisper the words.

Around them, the room had grown darker where a few candles were snuffed out to heighten the intimacy. *Damn Jane.*

Henry's body tightened and his hands clenched with the

urge to reach out and haul Lily firmly against him. *Damn her, too.* With one kiss, she'd reawakened everything he'd hope to forget about her.

Still, she had not moved one inch in his direction. He cleared his throat, and she jumped. At last, she reached out to grasp the lapel of his jacket. With agonizing slowness, she shifted closer, his heart beating faster with each short step. Her trembling fingers fumbled for the silk item, and part of him regretted not burying it deeper inside his pocket. She smelled faintly of violets, sweet and sensual. With her dark hair tickling his chin, he drew the aromatic scent of her skin into his lungs.

He bent his head to murmur against her right ear, "I'd much prefer your way of confiscating things off my person," he said, reminding her of the kiss she'd surrendered to him earlier.

"Pompous."

He chuckled, continually amazed at her unguarded responses.

She stepped back, her cheeks tinted with a blush.

"Now, gentlemen, take the handkerchief from your partner and place it over her eyes."

"I do wish I'd stayed upstairs," Lily murmured.

"And I wish I'd stayed with you." Her gaze lifted to his, and they stared at each other for a quiet moment. On an exhale, she handed him the blindfold and closed her eyes. With gentle hands, he wrapped the white linen around her silken hair. He imagined the soft strands cascading across his bare chest and suppressed an impassioned shudder.

"Is that too tight?" his voice sounded husky and strained.

She shook her head. "No, sir, but I'm not sure I want to do this." Her words trembled. For a woman who'd kissed him without shame or inhibition, she seemed suddenly shy and unsure. To be honest, he wasn't certain he wanted her to do this either. After all, the woman he'd brought here stood only a few feet away.

"Now twirl your partner around five times, let her go, and step back five paces."

With reluctant hands, Henry did as his sister instructed.

"Ladies, the first gentleman you touch will remain your new partner for the rest of the evening."

Henry snapped his head in Jane's direction, infuriated. Just when he'd resigned himself to staying in Miss Scott's company, his sister had gone and changed the rules so that Lily would go to someone else. And, as it appeared, that someone else was his damnable friend, Waverley.

Chapter Four

Henry had been so distracted with his closest friend's delighted reaction to the turn of events regarding Lily that he didn't notice who'd found him until she wrapped her arms around his neck, her breath heavy in his right ear.

"Is that you, Mr. Dalton?"

"Yes, Miss Appleton. 'Tis I," he said, untangling her arms, and placing her a foot away.

The rest of the night, he took turns glaring alternately at his sister and his friend. He also followed Waverley and Lily with Miss Appleton's hand glued to his right sleeve. He supposed he might have acted a bit possessively, but the only thing Waverley loved more than women was getting them alone. Just like he was doing right now.

"Is it not too late for a walk in the garden, Mr. Dalton?" Miss Appleton asked, her pace hurried, trying to keep up with him.

"No," he answered, grabbing a candle off the closest mantelpiece and exiting through the French doors. Outside, he remained several yards behind Waverley and his new partner, trying to catch their conversation, all the while having Miss Appleton buzz in his ear about the latest balls in London.

"Do you not agree, Mr. Dalton?"

"What? Oh…yes, of course."

Miss Appleton smiled, apparently oblivious to Henry's inattention to her chatter. Ahead of them, Lily giggled, her musical laugh lifting into the rustling treetops. When Waverley rotated her around, Henry could not help but notice her gaiety disappear the moment her gaze fell upon his.

He continued to walk toward her, consumed by emotions he'd not allowed himself to feel until now. His blood rushed inside his veins, causing his heart to beat at a wild and unsteady pace. Tightening his fists, he tried to quell the rising desire to kiss her again. What made him falter was wondering whether she might have another letter tucked in her sleeve. His gaze fell there before rising slowly back to her beguiling face.

In the dancing candlelight, he saw her blush. When they passed each other, he sent her a curt nod, and she graced him with a curious smile. A small breeze kicked up, sending the delicious smell of her skin swirling in the warm night air. He wanted to talk to her again, to say something to strike up a conversation. Thus far, Miss Appleton had changed subjects four times, each one managing to bore him more than the last.

"I hear your sister's friend, Miss Prescott—"

"Her name is Miss Scott."

"I thought you introduced her as—"

"We both know you were aware of her actual name before you arrived, Miss Appleton, despite my unwarranted introduction."

The woman reacted to his brusque reply with an annoying pout.

"Forgive me and please do go on about Miss Scott." It seemed Miss Appleton's sole purpose in life was to know everyone and the rumors attached to their name.

"Very well. Miss *Scott*, I've heard, will be married soon to a gentleman whose good looks far exceed his character."

Henry felt the muscle in his jaw jump. Of course, he already knew this. He'd had the misfortune of playing cards with the incorrigible fop several months ago. While John Gibbons was exceedingly handsome, the man was also a drunk and a gambler. Under the influence of brandy, he had bragged about marrying a woman whose father was willing to pay off his debts. When Henry had discovered the unfortunate woman was Miss Scott, he'd just sat there, his mind unable to comprehend her married to anyone but—

"She could do worse, I suppose," Miss Appleton said, flipping her fan out to cast a gentle breeze on her face.

Henry had to force his teeth apart. As a boy, he had loved Lily like no other. They had been young, barely old enough to contemplate a future, but she'd listened to his wild dreams of one day owning more land than his father.

The seasons flew by, changing them and his feelings for her. Although he'd always been protective of Lily, hence Jane's innocent and playful marriage vows, his mind and body had grown more enamored and more aware of her. Eventually, his father had noticed this, pulling him aside and informing him of the importance of marrying well.

Miss Scott, though amiable and handsome, does not possess the amount needed to keep Hadley from falling to creditors, and so should not be considered as a marital prospect.

She would also not bring Henry enough to be able to purchase more land like he'd always wanted. Realizing his duty and being too young to argue, Henry had forced himself to forget all about her. He moved to London soon afterward where he met women who loved to flirt and teach him the art of lovemaking. He remained enamored of their attention until he fell in lust with a green-eyed, genteel woman who'd neglected to tell him she was already married. Fortunately for him, the selfish woman's husband was drunk and a terrible shot.

Furious with himself and the turn of events in his life, he drank himself into a stupor and staggered home, only to stumble upon his mother wrapped in another man's arms. It was a devastating discovery, one that caused him to quit Hadley Manor for good. His respect for all women shattered, he vowed only to return home when he knew his parents were in Bath.

This time, he was aware of Lily visiting and supposed, or rather hoped, she no longer mattered to him. He came seeking closure, to prove she was the same as every woman he knew, flirtatious and untrustworthy. So far, she was doing a damn good job of proving him right on both accounts.

"That was a lovely walk, Mr. Dalton."

Henry shook himself and glanced down to find Miss Appleton still clinging mercilessly to his arm. Inside the manor, he spied Lily and Waverley talking and smiling at one another. He strode toward them, Miss Appleton in tow.

"Ah, Dalton, it is a fantastic night, isn't it? And just look at Miss Scott. I dare say, that walk in the garden brought a spectacular glow to her cheeks."

Tossed into a bad mood over his thoughts, Henry didn't care to guard his words. "Are you saying there wasn't a glow in Miss Scott's face earlier, Waverley?

Beside him, Miss Appleton tilted her head to glare at his profile. He was sure he'd just offended her by keeping Miss Scott the center of their conversation. Again, he didn't care.

Waverley shook his head. "Why, no of course. That's not…what I implied at all."

Henry sliced a glance toward Lily, whose dark eyebrows rose over her flashing green eyes.

"Please do not worry yourself, Mr. Waverley," she said,

her gentle hand on his sleeve. "I took your words as a compliment. Since it is most likely that Mr. Dalton here is unfamiliar with providing such praise, it is evident that he did not recognize it for what it was."

Waverley, this time, nodded his head at a vigorous rate. "Oh, oh very well, then, I…I suppose."

"Oh, lovely, what are we all talking about?" Jane said, springing up behind them.

Still annoyed at his sister, Henry sent her a warning glance. She only smiled and focused her full attention on Waverley.

"I apologize, but I must steal your partner from you, sir, is that all right?"

"Well…I'm—"

"Very well," she said, smiling wide enough to crinkle the delicate skin around her blue eyes.

His patience worn, Henry caught his sister by the elbow and pulled her back to whisper into her right ear. "What are you plotting, Jane?"

She lifted her shoulders in a slight shrug and whispered back to him. "You must keep on your toes, dear brother, for there is a surprise waiting around every corner."

Chapter Five

Lily lay in bed the next morning, after talking way past midnight to Jane about the night's events. Lily thought it curious how her friend didn't ask about the letter or mention Mr. Waverley at all in their conversation. She only wanted to know what Lily thought of Henry.

Pompous. Unnerving. Impossible. Insufferable.

Since then, Lily's mind had remained in turmoil over her heart's reignited feelings for Jane's brother. How she'd remained so in love with him for so long, she didn't know. Maybe she'd clung to his vow to avoid growing up and accepting the responsibilities placed before her. Since seeing him again and having more than a one-word conversation—or, more accurately, a stuttered nervous greeting—she realized he had not only said their wedding vows in jest but also continued to mock their acquaintance at every turn. Miss Prescott, indeed.

Heartbroken, she let the tears fall from her eyes to wet the hair at her temples. "I do not love you," she said, hiccupping the last word. Soon, she'd marry as her parents had done, for convenience, and carry on as her mother had done, bearing children and plotting ways to marry them off.

Her thoughts then turned to Mr. Gibbons. She'd met him only three times, each one revealing a new truth about his character. Though handsome, he possessed a quick temper and a love of Port. She wondered, however, if she had not given him a fair chance, always comparing him to Henry, the boy she'd married on a blistering day in August.

Reconciled to accepting what fate handed her, Lily lifted out of bed and dressed, determined to treat Henry Dalton with as much triviality as he'd treated her.

****

Henry tried not to glance up at the drawing room entranceway every time he heard a soft footstep. Lily had yet to show herself, and Miss Appleton's constant whining about the warmth in the elaborate space was testing his civility toward her.

"Since it looks like rain," his sister said, "I have decided we need another parlor game to keep us occupied."

The room clapped in agreement, and Henry smiled. The corner of his mouth lifted higher when he saw Lily in the doorway, dark tendrils framing her bright face, her light-green empire gown bringing out the olive tone of her skin. When his pulse quickened, he realized the kiss they'd shared had done nothing but stir his blood, so that the craving to kiss her again consumed him.

On a discreet exhale, he stood to welcome her approach, with Miss Appleton attached.

"Miss Scott."

Her gaze lifted to his eyes before dropping down to his mouth. His heart kicked against his ribs, stealing a breath.

He didn't know how long they stared at each other before Miss Appleton nudged him and asked, "Are you unwell, sir?"

"No. I'm quite well," he answered without saying anything more.

The woman harrumphed and swung away from him.

His heart continued to pound until Jane brought over a black velvet bag and rattled it close to Lily's chest.

"It's the ladies' turn to pick their partner," she said, smiling.

He didn't miss the subtle shake of Lily's head or the new sadness in her eyes. He wondered what had happened between their last conversation and now. He believed he didn't have to wonder long, not with Jane plotting to bring them back together.

"You must, dear. If you don't play, it will be uneven," Jane said.

Henry waited until Lily reached in and pulled out the card with his name on one side.

"I…I have Mr. Waverley."

"What?" Henry exclaimed, causing everyone to glance in his direction. He shook his head and dismissed them with a scowl and a wave of his hand. He stepped toward his sister to protest when Miss Appleton reached her hand into the accursed bag, pulled out the parchment, and projected his name across the great room.

He halted, glancing toward Lily whose fine features were pulled into soft, perplexed lines. *Damn.* Henry had no idea whether one should protest the outcome of the cards. He remained silent, nonetheless, while the other two women continued to pull names from the bag and Waverley sauntered up to Lily, a wide grin on his face.

"Would you like to play a game of cards, Mr. Dalton?" In a polite manner, Henry unwrapped himself from Miss Appleton's ensnarling hands and stalked to confront Jane. "Why did you have Miss Scott receive Waverley's name and not mine?" He'd known for years the game wasn't as *random* as Jane had everyone believe.

His sister sighed. "Because, dear brother, the last time you were *matched* with Miss Scott, I was scolded thoroughly for it. Besides, Mr. Waverley is enamored with her, and I could not let a good game go to waste."

"Waverley is enamored with anything with an ample bosom," he said between clenched teeth.

"Oh, I didn't know you took time to look at Miss Scott's ample—"

"There was a time, Jane when I was resigned not to think about her, much less look at the woman at all."

"Mr. Dalton?"

Henry rotated around to find Miss Appleton pouting. "Have I done something to upset you, sir?"

Henry let out an irritated sigh. "No, Miss Appleton. I was just clarifying something with my sister. Shall we?" He offered the woman his arm and led her to an empty settee near the dreary, rain-soaked window.

Around him, conversations hummed, with Miss Putnam

casting seductive glances at him when William Naughton wasn't looking. There was also Miss Carrington, who always seemed to pull Harry Bentley's card, a trick his sister had perfected over the years. Henry had no doubt they would be married within the fortnight.

While the women were all handsome, Henry's gaze kept wandering to Lily, who appeared at ease with Waverley, even with him peering shamelessly at her chest every time she inhaled.

"The devil," Henry swore under his breath.

"I beg your pardon?" Miss Appleton said.

Henry shook his head, drawing from her an indignant lungful of air.

"Excuse me, Mr. Dalton," she said, hesitating, he supposed, to see if he'd stop her.

He bowed and she sighed, twisting away from him. Across the room, he found Lily, reading a collection of prose, alone. He didn't go to her right away, taking his time so as not to attract any more attention to them. She curtsied on his subtle approach.

"How are you finding Mr. Waverley's company, madam?" Henry asked, wishing he'd thought to inquire about the weather instead.

"Obliging," she said, her mouth lifting slightly at the corners.

He stared down at her. "Well, that sounds dull."

"On the contrary, Mr. Dalton." Her smile widened, and he wondered how he'd been able to stay away from her for so many years. After leaving Hadley, he'd allowed the spark of curiosity and interest to remain lit, believing time and distance would allow his love for her to snuff itself out. He had been mistaken. Seeing her again, kissing her again, he wondered how much more he could take before that growing spark formed into a ravenous fire.

Fortunately, he didn't have time to ponder the answer. Miss Appleton, in dramatic fashion, returned with a book clasped in her hands.

Beside him, Lily made a small strangled sound that caused him to glance in her direction. Her face, once pink and healthy, was drained of so much color that he thought he might have to save her from dropping dead away from a faint.

"Miss Dalton, I just happened upon this book of romantic plays. How about we act out a few of them?"

As the crowd clapped their approval, Jane lifted her gaze in Lily's direction, the two women staring at each other for a frantic moment.

"I…uhm…"

Henry witnessed the peculiar exchange with heightened awareness. Was the compilation his sister's or Lily's? If it did belong to one of them, neither made an attempt to take it back into their possession.

"I believe a play would be a marvelous change," Waverley interjected, receiving a happy smile from Miss Appleton.

"Who's in favor?"

Everyone except for Jane and Lily said "aye."

"It is unanimous," Miss Appleton quipped.

Outnumbered, Jane selected the scene the "actors" would

perform, proceeding to call out the cast of characters. There were in fact only two. "There is a Miss Gravehart who appears to be in love with a Mr. Mortimer."

Henry shifted his gaze to Lily, finding her eyes closed and her hands clasped together at her waist. He felt compelled to engage her once again, this time, drawing close enough so their bodies almost touched. "Do you like plays, Miss Scott?"

She jumped at the sound of his voice and exhaled before spinning around to blink her large eyes at him. He smiled down at her, his gaze wandering to her moist, plump, and slightly parted lips. He had to chuckle to himself. He'd yet to find the recipient of her amorous letter, and now he was enveloped in another mystery.

As if on cue, Miss Appleton summarized the play from twelve feet away. His gaze never left Lily's face the entire time.

"It appears our heroine has had her heart broken by the gentleman and believes one kiss will either unbreak her heart or make it easier for her to break his."

"How very trite, don't you agree, Miss Scott?"

Lily inhaled and then let out a quick, impatient breath. "I agree that you are one of the most cynical men I've ever met," she whispered back at him.

Once enamored with him, or so he'd thought, now she seemed to struggle to tolerate him. Still, even when they were arguing, he believed there was no other place he'd rather be than with her.

"I'm very sorry to disappoint you, but I'm neither cynical nor heartbroken. I am, however, disenchanted enough to believe love is not some fairytale." He paused to lean in closer to her right ear. "Nor is it a whimsical play made up by a woman who would rather bring two fictional characters together than pursue a love of her own."

Chapter Six

Lily squeezed her hands into fists. How she ever thought herself in love with Mr. Henry Dalton, she didn't know. "You are so sure that a woman wrote it, sir?"

His eyebrows lifted over his steel-gray eyes, unnerving her further. She could only wait in furious silence for his reply.

"Yes. Men don't believe in trapping themselves, and if they did, they surely wouldn't write a play, giving a woman the idea of how to go about doing it."

She scoffed, distracted from the mortification of having her compilation read out loud to a group of men and women, some of whom she'd only just met. "Please, Mr. Dalton, must you voice everything you think aloud? It's quite depressing."

His mouth opened, but he only managed to stare down at her until she twisted around, determined to ignore him. Since Henry had come to stand close to her, she'd been unable to concentrate, much less comprehend how Miss Appleton had found her plays. For the sake of remaining anonymous, however, she had to keep quiet and composed.

"I believe I should play Miss Gravehart and Mr. Dalton should play Mr. Mortimer," Miss Appleton pronounced across the room.

"Oh, dear God," Henry mumbled behind Lily's back. If she hadn't been so ready to faint, she might have laughed.

Jane, to Lily's relief, rose to salvage the disastrous turn of events. "I dare say, Miss Appleton, you are too bold in your requests. Since I am the hostess here, I shall make up the rules, and I say there will be a drawing to see who plays Miss Gravehart and Mr. Mortimer. Are there any objections?"

Lily glanced around, along with everyone else.

"Very well. I shall write 'Miss Gravehart' on one piece of

paper and 'Mr. Mortimer' on another. The rest shall remain blank. Whoever draws the two characters will rehearse and then perform before my guests."

Of the men, Henry alone refused to draw a card. The winner, of sorts, turned out to be Mr. Waverley. Lily thought of refusing to draw, as well, until she began to fear Henry would assume she wasn't playing because he wasn't playing. *Pompous.*

So, she pulled the card and bent her head, finding the familiar name scribbled on the front.

"It's all right, Lily," Jane assured her with a smile. Lily didn't know what to think of her friend's relationship with Mr. Waverley anymore. It appeared not even to exist.

"Is this what you've hoped for, Miss Scott? To play Mr. Waverley's lover?" Henry leaned down to whisper.

She turned and blinked at him for a good moment. If she allowed herself to, she might think him jealous. She inhaled and smiled. "Yes, sir. Since I met your friend, less than twenty-four hours ago, I've had visions of entrapping him in a loveless marriage where we should aspire to have thirteen children, most of them boys, one of whom we are sure to name after you!"

They glared at each other, her heart pounding with frustration and from the warmth of his breath glancing across her skin. Then, she curtsied and left him to join Mr. Waverley.

****

Henry's gaze followed Lily's soft gait while his mind contemplated a dozen ways to get her alone. He still hadn't guessed the person to whom she had written the letter, though he'd agonized over the recipient's identity the entire night. Although she'd tried to distract him from guessing Waverley, Henry still was not convinced his friend had nothing to do with the damn thing.

My Love,

You may have thought of me only once or twice; yet, I have thought of you for what seems all my life. With one slight gaze in your direction, I am lost. I know it seems impossible for me to confess such things, to express an affection that has been

unrequited. However, you must know, I have loved you and only

you.

Perhaps, he thought, if a kiss was used to retrieve the

letter, a kiss might be needed to reveal to whom the letter was

written. He just had to know the man who inspired such passion,

such ardent feelings.

"Oh, but Mr. Dalton, I wanted us to play the two

characters." Miss Appleton suddenly appeared to drone next to his

left elbow.

He shook his head. "Why?"

To Henry's satisfaction, the woman remained struck by

his question, her speechlessness making him smile.

"As I thought." He nodded a dismissal. "Now if you will

excuse me, I'm in need of a good drink."

He took his time to go and pour himself a generous

amount of brandy before falling in behind a row of chairs beside the mantelpiece, glaring at the couple rehearsing across the drawing room.

"I don't believe I like the idea of Lily kissing Mr. Waverley."

This time it was Jane who had approached without Henry noticing. "He seems overcome by her to the point that he may indeed ask for her hand before we have finished supper."

Henry withdrew the glass from his lips and glanced down at his sister, her mouth pulled tight with anxiety.

"Waverley is irrational, but he's not a fool." He meant to set his sister at ease with those words. He meant to set himself at ease, as well.

But Jane sucked in a lungful of air. "Are you saying one would have to be a fool to marry Miss Scott? No wonder she had nothing good to say about you last night."

His sister stepped to walk away when he took hold of her upper arm and gently pulled her back toward him. "What did she say about me?"

Jane made a face and rolled her cornflower-blue eyes. "Let's see, I believe pompous, impossible, insufferable, and..." She paused to tap her chin with her index finger. "Well, I can't remember the other one, but it wasn't enjoyable or amiable. Of that, I'm quite sure."

He drew back, the vein in his temple beginning to throb at how many unpleasant things Lily had said about him while he lay in bed, reliving every moment in her company.

"She doesn't deserve your ire, Henry. Whoever you're angry with, I would suggest you address it with her instead of taking it out on Miss Scott."

Jane sashayed away, leaving Henry to want to quit the entire place altogether. He twisted toward the door when his motion gained Miss Appleton's attention. Before a few days ago, he'd had no intention of seeing her again. Their brief affair had ended months ago. Still, he wanted, or rather, needed a recreational diversion. So far, she'd done nothing but annoy him. Of course, that wasn't her fault. His diversions, he found, lay elsewhere and with someone else.

"Oh, Mr. Dalton, I cannot tell you how disappointed I am that we are not the ones rehearsing at this very moment."

"So you've said. So, let us count our blessings. It could be you and Mr. Waverley and me and Miss Scott."

As he expected, Miss Appleton wrinkled her pert nose. "You and Miss Scott? Why, surely, you would have protested such a fate?"

His eyes narrowed, pushing the woman back a pace. Since he'd been less than cordial to her for the past day or so, he didn't know if she was acting desperate, oblivious, or both. "Whatever do you mean?"

Miss Appleton sent him a forced smiled and blinked her lashes. "Only that Miss Scott has both vexed and fascinated you from the moment you first saw her. From where I stand, you have vexed and fascinated her, too. I'm just curious as to why?"

Henry exhaled and glanced over to where Waverley stood close to Lily, his finger lifted to brush back a lock of her dark hair. Fire shot through Henry's veins, rapacious and consuming. Had all this come from one kiss? *No.* His want had started a few years ago, building at a maddening pace and beyond his control.

Jane popped up before him and Miss Appleton. "Henry, will you assist Mr. Waverley in moving the couches? For the scene, their backs must touch."

Shaken, Henry grasped at a chance to ignore Miss Appleton's question and talk to Waverley, the sod. He stalked at a determined pace toward the man, stopping out of general earshot of everyone in the room. "So, how do you feel performing with Miss Scott?"

Waverley glanced up and smiled. "Fortunate."

The answer kicked Henry in the stomach, and he couldn't help but make the impact worse by striding the short distance to where Waverley's partner stood. Uncaring of how it appeared, he reached out to grasp her arm in a firm hold. "Is this what you mean to do, madam, to make a mockery out of yourself?"

She lifted her chin and gazed into his face, her green eyes

bright with unspoken emotions. "I'm doing no such thing. It's a play, Mr. Dalton, and if you find you cannot watch the performance, you are free to go."

She pulled away, leaving him frozen in place. Twenty feet away, she and Waverley sat down on the couch while the audience gathered in high-backed chairs. Resigned to watch, Henry leaned against the mantelpiece, his jaw clenched and his gaze never leaving Lily's face.

With the wet day casting a dim light on the room, everyone waited for the play to begin.

"It is a lovely evening so far, Mr. Mortimer, is it not?"

Waverley smiled, but his chin remained elevated as if her company were beneath his. "Let's not waste our time tonight with trite conversation, Miss Gravehart."

Lily bent her head to her hands. "That's right, sir. Forgive me. I forgot how you are a man who doesn't waste time with women of my station. I also know you have little patience with triviality in life or with idle conversation."

Waverley rotated in dramatic fashion toward Miss Scott. "No, I'm a man who knows what he wants."

"God, he's atrocious, isn't he," Henry muttered, causing Jane to spin around and shush him.

The play continued with Lily lowering her voice to a smooth, seductive whisper. "I must ask, though, does what you want, include me, Mr. Mortimer?"

Henry straightened from his languished stance. At the same time, the small audience gasped in surprise at her question.

"It appears your boldness has caused a few eavesdroppers to suck in a large amount of air, Miss Gravehart. Perhaps my coming all this way was a mistake."

"Are you saying that the few instances of intimate conversation, the night that we danced, not one, but three dances together, were also mistakes, Mr. Mortimer?"

Henry pulled forward; surprised he wanted to know Waverley's answer. Of course, in continued dramatic fashion, Waverley shot up from his seat. In a blink, Lily stood to block his path, her hands reaching out to stop him.

"You loved me once, sir. Don't you remember?"

"No, I did not love you, Miss Gravehart. It was you who loved me."

Henry sliced a glance toward the audience, observing as everyone held their breath. When he twisted back to Lily, her hand was raised and caressing Waverley's enamored face.

"Yes, sir, I did love you."

Henry could only stare as she lifted on her tiptoes and touched her lips to the side of Waverley's mouth. She pulled away, blinking, a stray tear caught in her long lashes and glittering in a single candle's flickering light. Henry's heart squeezed inside his chest.

"I am to be married tomorrow, sir, and after today, I shall never think of you again," she said, shifting to kiss the other side of Waverley's mouth.

The room remained cloaked in silence. After a few moments, Henry realized Waverley had forgotten his godforsaken lines. Jane, in heroic fashion, glanced down at the book, leaned forward, and whispered the line in the man's direction.

"Alas, it's just—"

Waverley jerked out of his stupor, causing the women to snicker. "Yes, yes of course. Alas, it's just as well since…since…"

Jane whispered again. "Since we have—"

"Since we have nothing in—"

His patience spent, Henry stalked toward his sister, plucked the book from her hand and strode to where Waverley stood, shoving him out of the way. Henry didn't miss the glow of rage in Lily's face as he stepped close, his gaze half on her, half on the neatly printed words.

"Since we have nothing in common except the kiss we shared, madam."

Chapter Seven

Lily had never wanted to smack another human so hard in her entire life. Henry Dalton had done nothing but cause her grief since he'd stolen her heart right from underneath her seven odd years ago.

"Must you ruin every one of my aspirations?" she said, unable to keep in character.

"And which aspiration would that be this time, Miss Scott? Is it kissing a man so thoroughly that he is left powerless and can think of nothing but finding a way to solicit another?"

In the deafening silence, Jane softly projected, "she's Miss Gravehart."

Lily, aggrieved and shocked by Henry's words that were

nowhere in her play, could only lash out in a low tone. "Do you not see any fault in what you do, Mr. Dalton?"

"He's Mr. Mortimer," Jane corrected her.

Henry's chin lifted as if his white cravat had become too tight around his neck. "I see only a woman who cannot decide if she wants to marry or remain a flirt all of her life."

Ungloved, Lily reached up and slapped Henry across his handsome, pompous face. The sound echoed between the small audience, past Mr. Waverley and out the doors into the foyer. The crack even jerked Aunt Sophia awake, her loud snort causing an obnoxious ricochet.

In the humming silence that followed, Lily stared at Henry's reddened cheek before lifting her gaze to his hard, steel-gray eyes. Her palm stung from the impact, and her throat hurt from years of unshed tears. "How dare you assume anything about me, sir, when you have made no effort to speak to me for more than two minutes, once a year at most, since we were—"

She halted her tongue, causing his head to tilt at an

intrigued angle. "Since we were what?"

She exhaled, dropping her shoulders in a defeated manner. "It doesn't matter," she said, curtsying, and spinning toward the audience. An enthusiastic round of applause followed her departure from the room and into the wet afternoon. She needed air, and she needed to be alone.

She walked the soggy path toward the line of yews by a nearby pond, her body shaking with disbelief and disappointment. The air hung thick and wet, chilling her bare skin and what remained of her pride. On a neglected bench, behind an arching dog-rose bush, she sank down. She wished she'd never come to Hadley Manor or accepted Jane's invitation. Although the banns had not been read, Lily had allowed her father to encourage John Gibbons to pursue her hand. She would marry Mr. Gibbons to unburden her parents, and he would marry her to unburden his pockets.

A sob tore from her throat at the prospect of such a loveless future. Lily supposed if she had not stood before God and nature all those years ago and promised herself to one particular man, her gaze blurred with fanciful innocence, she might not care whom she married at this point.

"You will catch your death if you do not come back inside."

Lily glanced up to find Mr. Waverley standing beside her, his light hair damp and darker across his forehead.

"You should not be here," she said to him. She was unaccompanied, and he was a single man whom she'd kissed not more than ten minutes ago. All anyone needed to do was speculate, and she would be calling herself Mrs. Waverley and not Mrs. Gibbons or Mrs. Dalton.

"May I?" he asked, stretching out his hand toward the empty seat beside her.

She nodded, unable to deny him. He sat down, his motions slow and meticulous. She tried concentrating on the quiet tap of water as it fell from one pink dog-rose petal to another, a few feet away.

"I heard Dalton speak of you once, several years ago," he said, staring straight ahead, his profile more striking, now that she had a chance to view his face in the filtered afternoon light. His sideburns were shorter than what was in style but still longer than Henry's.

"I'm sure you are mistaken, sir."

Mr. Waverley twisted on the bench toward her, his gaze stern but soft. "When he's in his cups, he's a different person, and he recites the most horrid poetry anyone can ever imagine."

Lily giggled in spite of herself. What a glorious thing to imagine after she'd just experienced the very worst of him.

"Of course, he does say a few lines that are memorable. My favorite will always remain about the maid with forest-green eyes and dark-brown hair, her lips like silk, her name a flower."

Waverley lifted his gaze to her face before dropping it back to her mouth. She froze, her heart tumbling over in her chest.

"Don't worry, I'm not going to kiss you," he said, pausing to bring in a deep breath. "I'm not a scoundrel, although life would be much more fun if I were."

Lily had to admit, Mr. Waverley did have the most adorable pout. When he stood, he reached out his arm for her to take. "Now, I have been summoned by Miss Dalton to come and fetch you from this dreary afternoon. If I return without you, she has promised to put dear Aunt Sophia's name inside the bowl for me to draw."

Lily laughed and stood, resting her palm upon his sleeve. As they rotated around to walk the muddy path back to the house, she paused. "Mr. Waverley, I was…under the impression, you and Jane were—"

He threw back his head and laughed. When he'd sobered, he tugged his arm gently to get her to start walking again. "Oh, I do adore Henry's sister, that is clear, but she is too occupied, and I am too single-minded."

Mr. Waverley's confession was not what Lily expected to hear, not with a letter tucked under her pillow intended for him. "Are you sure?"

This time, he halted. "Why?"

Lily exhaled and shook her head. "I just thought…with both of you being so…handsome and amiable—"

He chuckled, showing a tiny dimple on his right cheek. "For now we are both satisfied to toy with one another, remaining free and careless with our feelings."

Left more confused, and with the air growing muggier by the minute, Lily merely smiled and stepped back inside the large manor with its marble-tiled entrance hall, grand parlor, and ornate plastered ceilings. Everything about Hadley boasted an importance of finery and wealth. Although the Scotts had a modest income, to some extent, it didn't compare to the Daltons' or how they chose to live. She believed the only reason she was allowed to "play" with Jane was that their grandmothers were close friends who had ended up marrying on different ends of the social spectrum.

Once settled in the parlor, Lily began—discreetly, of course—searching for her book of plays. The rest of the afternoon had her visiting every room at Hadley Manor that wasn't locked. By early evening, she'd deduced that Mr. Dalton, wherever he was, still held on to them. Of course, she soon discovered, he had also left Hadley Manor, for a quick ride to survey the land he was to one day inherit.

"It's my guess he will keep riding north, unlikely to return," Jane said with a sigh. "Oh, I don't know what has possessed my brother to make him so disagreeable these last few days."

Lily clamped down on her lips, unwilling to divulge the fact Jane's brother had read the letter Lily had written to Mr. Waverley and had assumed the very worst.

"What's the matter, Lily? You've grown quite pale. Are you ill?"

Lily shook her head. "No, Jane. I'm just…I'm a little confused about you and Mr. Waverley. When you asked me to write the letter, I assumed there was an ardent regard between the two of you. Since that time, you have allowed me to be his partner and then sat, without protest, while I proceeded to kiss him in the play."

Jane's smile widened. "That reminds me; I meant to ask you about his lips."

"Jane!" Lily exclaimed, a little too loudly. She cleared her throat and guided her friend away from Aunt Sophia. Out of earshot, Lily asked her question.

"I'm wondering, after spending some time with Mr. Waverley in the garden," Lily continued, trying to keep her voice from carrying, "if I should consider tearing up the love letter I wrote to him?"

Her friend's smile disappeared, her gaze diverted to a spot just above Lily's right shoulder. A cold wave of realization sliced up Lily's spine as she recognized the cause of Jane's distraction was, without a doubt, the sudden appearance of Henry Dalton.

Chapter Eight

"I suppose I should be surprised, but I'm not."

Lily squeezed her eyes shut for a moment before rotating to find Henry's steely gaze bearing down on her. She supposed, to keep him from judging her, she could have called Jane out, thus subjecting Mr. Waverley to a duel with his best friend.

But the last thing Lily wanted to see was a bullet hole in Mr. Waverley's dimpled cheek. So instead, she smiled and hoped, one day, Jane and Mr. Waverley might name a child after her. "There is something to be said, Mr. Dalton, about eavesdropping on a lady's private conversation."

One dark eyebrow shot up. "And there is something to be said, Miss Scott, about perverse indiscretion."

Lily's fingers curled inside her palms. He was the most intolerable man she'd ever met. "I'd thought you'd left, sir, unlikely to return."

His scowl softened, his smirking lips lifting to wreak havoc on her intolerant nerves. "I had some—" His gaze dropped to her mouth. "—unfinished business here."

Lily's heart flipped and then sank. There he stood, calling her perverse and indiscreet, all the while plotting ways to compromise her character. Oh, she could only guess what he had in mind for her. For the first time since he'd discarded their friendship, or whatever one would like to call it, she mourned their innocence and the love she'd once felt for him. Now, it might do her well to quit Hadley Manor and tell her father to have the reading of the banns placed for her and Mr. Gibbons, directly. First, however, she needed to get her book of plays back from Henry, without him discovering she wrote them. A kiss would not work this time.

"Since the weather has vastly improved, I say, we should

all go for a walk," Jane announced, stirring Aunt Sophia out of her slumber.

"Marvelous idea, Miss Dalton," Mr. Waverley said, coming up behind them. "And before you think about us drawing names, I claim Miss Scott here as my walking partner."

Lily didn't know who to glance toward first, so she kept her gaze on Mr. Waverley, his dimpled smile infectious.

"And I would like Mr. Dalton to escort me through the garden," Miss Appleton projected a few feet away.

"Then it is settled," Jane declared and clapped, rousing the other couples from their card game.

"Shall we?" Mr. Waverley asked, leaning down to offer Lily his arm. He was taller than Henry and thinner, not to mention far more polite and amiable. He was beginning to grow on her as well.

"We shall," she said, smiling and sliding past Miss Appleton and her disgruntled escort on their way to the foyer. Into the dissipating heat of the early evening, they ambled down a pebbled walkway, past a line of white peonies. They had lasted longer this year, through the end of July. On their way by, Mr. Waverley picked her a blooming flower, twisting the short stem between his long fingers before handing it to her.

They engaged in small talk about the weather, the season, and his estate in Oxfordshire.

"I should invite you there this autumn, Miss Scott, and we shall go for long walks and talk about absolutely nothing at all," he said, his voice raised and his tone enthusiastic.

Lily suspected she'd be married by the end of summer, unable to visit anyone—even her parents—for a long time. "I'd like that very much, sir," she said, a tinge of sadness in her voice.

Behind them, she heard the steady footfall of Henry's Hessian boots and the crunch of pebbles under Miss Appleton's voluptuous form. Lily remained so alert to their conversation about the latest gossip of the Duke and Duchess of Devonshire that she didn't notice an aggressive mother swan until it spread its beautiful wings and hissed toward Lily.

In dramatic fashion, Mr. Waverley, who must have thought her in danger, wrapped his arms around her waist and tried cautioning them to step backward. They had gone only two paces when her foot found a three-inch hole, causing her to lose her balance, taking Mr. Waverley right along with her. Lily landed on top of him, his arms still around her waist and his hands splayed upon her back. Blinking, she stared down at his striking face, his heart pounding against hers.

"They can be quite hostile," he said, his blue eyes wide, his words breathless across her heated cheeks.

"Well, that was exciting to watch." Lily lifted her head to find Miss Appleton bent toward them; her delicate eyebrows cocked in amusement. Behind her, Henry stood, his head raised at a haughty angle and the muscle in his strong jaw flexing with unspoken words.

Convinced he had assumed she'd somehow plotted this entire clumsy scene, Lily pushed herself up, with Mr. Waverley's awkward help. Only, when she placed her right foot down, an unbearable pain sliced through her ankle, forcing her to grab the closest object to her: Mr. Waverley. Thrown off balance, she slammed against him, the intermingling of their bodies making him grunt, a sound heard for at least a quarter of a mile.

"You're hurt," Mr. Waverley said, his voice husky, but full of concern.

"I...I think I...twisted my ankle," she whispered, trying to right herself. As Miss Appleton scoffed, Henry reached out to grasp Lily's elbow. With a firm grip, he pulled her away from Mr. Waverley, wrapped his arm around her waist and lifted her slightly off the ground

"What are you doing?" she asked, mortified.

"Saving you from gossip," he murmured in her right ear, his tone sending spirals of heat into her midsection. Whether he was saving her from gossip or from his friend's company, she was never given a chance to ask.

"Waverley, take Miss Appleton back to the house, and do try to keep her at an arm's distance and, perhaps, away from any troubling holes."

Miss Appleton sputtered in protest as Mr. Waverley did as he was instructed, his gaze unable to stay above her neckline.

"I shall go and prepare some tea," Jane said, picking up the hem of her dress and scurrying past the three couples and up the curved path.

When everyone had disappeared behind the row of tall yews, Lily shoved away from Henry, hobbling back to keep from putting pressure on her tender foot.

"I'm quite well," she said, pushing up a lock of thick hair that had come unpinned.

He nodded, clasped his hands behind his back, and smiled. "Show me."

Lily's mouth fell open. She was hoping he'd leave her to attend to Miss Appleton. "I beg your pardon?"

His smile widened. "If you're fine, Miss Scott, you will be able to walk on your right foot, without assistance."

Henry's sultry smirk was enough to make her scream and

swoon at the same time. Forced to demonstrate she could at least travel from one place to another without having his strong arms wrapped around her, she shifted her weight, drawing her left foot up to take a step. Only when she did, the familiar pain shot from her ankle to her hip, causing her knees to buckle under her.

The strong arms she was trying so hard to avoid swooped underneath her in an effortless, breathless motion. She lay in Henry's arms, staring into his concerned features.

"Just as I thought," he said, his long strides moving them down a narrow trail, in the opposite direction of the house.

"Where…where are you taking me?" She hoped he didn't hear the thumping of her heart over her halting words. He said nothing, continuing to carry her, the warm and heady smell of his skin rising above the sweet aroma of summer flowers along the uncharted path.

"You're not going to put me down, are you?"

"That's very observant of you, Miss Scott."

"So, it would be useless for me to protest?"

"Quite."

She bit down on her tongue, resigned to let him carry her off, alone. Unsure of what the next minute held, she tried to relax, remembering the last time he'd carried her. She'd kissed him, not a pure or innocent exchange of affection, but a kiss that made her lips tingle and her insides flutter.

"There's a cold spring up ahead," he said, pulling her into the present. "If you have a sprain, it will bring down the swelling."

He carried her another sixty feet before pivoting onto an ivy-laden path that opened into one of the most enchanting places she'd ever seen. Ahead of them, a ten-foot waterfall plunged into a clear, rocky stream.

"I never knew this existed," she said, enamored.

He sat her down on a moss-covered rock, bending over her to slip his hand inside the hem of her dress. He hiked up her skirts to her bare kneecap, and she sucked in a surprised breath.

"Mr. Dalton...I—" she said, fighting with him to pull her

dress toward her feet.

He exhaled as if he were dealing with an unruly child and shifted forward, his warm breath glancing over her cheeks. "Miss Scott, I've had the privilege of knowing the taste of your lips, so I do believe it's a little too late for modesty. Now, take off your boot."

She drew back at his brusque tone. "It would do you well to improve your manners regarding patient care, Mr. Dalton."

He sent her a sly smile, the simple gesture causing a thousand goose bumps to pop up all over her body. "Being that I'm not a doctor, nor do I aspire to become one, I will do no such thing. And, now that you've dallied too long, I'll do it for you."

Her protests futile, she allowed him to unlace her boot and gently guide her foot into the frigid water. Cold did not begin to describe the crisp and numbing stream lapping over her ankle. He held his palm upon her knee; she supposed to keep her from removing her ankle from the therapeutic water. The warmth of his skin took her mind off her discomfort.

After a few moments of peaceful silence, she sighed. "I'm…I'm surprised to find you back at Hadley Manor and not settled in London for the evening. What brought you back here?"

He sent her a rare smile, and for a moment, she recalled the innocence of their youth when he would chase her around the garden fountain, and she'd pretend to be out of breath so he'd catch her.

"If you must know, the answer to your question has changed in the last half hour. In fact, since learning, with great consternation, that Mr. Waverley is the inspiration behind your impassioned prolific letter, I've decided I should like to find a woman like you, Miss Scott, someone so overcome with my company that she forgets she is close to becoming engaged with another. Then, I believe, I would like to marry her."

Chapter Nine

Lily huffed, offended that he was mocking her without knowing the full truth. Yes, she was about to become engaged, but because she had no other choice. The opportunity for him to ask for her hand had come and gone.

"I wish I'd never written that letter. It was a mistake on all accounts. However, it cannot be undone. As for becoming engaged, it is not the same as being engaged. If you knew me well enough, Mr. Dalton, you'd know my devotion is unbreakable." *My heart, of course, is another matter.*

His gaze fell to hers, narrowed, and lifted away. "Oh, but I do know you well enough, Miss Scott. I'd like to say, I know you better than anyone here."

She dipped her chin to her chest, not missing the undertone of distrust and anger. She felt trapped, unable to tell him the truth about the letter, unable to accept the fact they had grown so far apart. There he sat contemplating his future with a woman, a wife, who was not her.

So rattled, she spoke her heart before he had the chance to stop her. "I don't understand how men can talk of marrying so carelessly, without the mention of ardent affection or love."

His head snapped up, drawing closer to hers. "Love is not a prerequisite to marriage, Miss Scott."

Lily sighed. "Oh, why do I bother having a conversation with you, when everything you have to say is so very disappointing?"

"It is not my intent to disappoint you in any way."

Oh, but he had. Despite the distance they'd placed between each other, and him taking every opportunity to anger her, she had never let herself imagine him marrying anyone else, until now. The thought made her shiver, prompting him to discard his jacket and drape it over her shoulders. She realized, since they'd kissed, there existed no more boundaries of propriety between them.

"Still, sir," she said, her heart starting to ache from the conversation, "you must admit that we live in the modern age where—"

"Where men marry for money and women for comfort? Yes, I admit it fully. For this reason, there should never be any cause for a woman and man to ever fall in love."

She twisted away at the passionate way he said the words. "Having a conversation with you, regarding the fancies of one's heart, can be so exhausting, Mr. Dalton."

He lifted his hand and brought his finger up to coax her face back to meet his. "So now I'm depressing, disappointing, and exhausting?"

She swallowed loudly and tried to keep her gaze from falling to his mouth. "That's not what I—"

He dropped his hand, straightened, and drew his knees, so

his elbows rested on them. Between his two thumbs and index fingers, he twiddled with a small twig. "No, no. Don't try to explain when it is, in all fairness, an accurate description of me. Even Jane has said it is so."

"And yet, you make no effort to change. Why?"

"Because I'm moderately wealthy, and I have all my teeth. I could be the most disreputable man in England and still have fifteen fathers lined up to introduce me to their daughters."

Her shoulders sank. "Like Miss Appleton?"

"Yes, just like Miss Appleton. She is handsome and accommodating."

"And you are handsome and, at times, disobliging. With one thing in common, perhaps you should consider becoming engaged to her."

His sideways smirk caused Lily's pulse to jump.

"You find me handsome, Miss Scott?"

"And disobliging," she reminded him.

He threw the twig into the rippling water and shifted

closer to her. She sucked in a quiet breath as he lifted his thumb to glide across her lower lip. Her heart, battered and bruised, beat at a quick and thunderous pace. She didn't understand how she could be in such a state of undress, discussing marriage, with Henry touching her as if they were the ones marrying each other.

"However, her father is only willing to part with her if I can assure him of remaining faithful 'til death do us part."

Lily harrumphed. "Now that this conversation has crossed all limits of impropriety, I cannot help but ask why you want to marry when you don't plan on remaining faithful to your wife."

His eyebrows rose over his mesmerizing gray eyes. "Oh, I certainly plan on doing so, madam. I just don't think it will be easy, not when I will be comparing her lips to yours, on every occasion."

Lily shook her head. "Oh, why must you tease me so?"

"Because I—"

His abrupt pause sent her pulse dancing. Did she dare guess what he was about to say? Or was she trying to find something in his unspoken words that wasn't there? All the same, a consuming fire spread to every part of her body, well, except her submerged foot. She closed her eyes and tried not to relive the moment when she'd kissed him or when he kissed her back. The vivid recollection of his lips so firm, his tongue like velvet, did nothing but make her long for him more.

"I believe it would be best to never bring up the subject of us…" She halted, opening her eyes, and finding the sunlight hitting the mist from the cascading waterfall, creating a bright rainbow across the polished rocks.

"What, madam?"

Lily shook her head. "You…and I…engaging in a …you know very well what we are not to speak of, Mr. Dalton."

With that, he dropped his hand and pulled away. "Yes, and then perhaps I wouldn't recall it as often," he mumbled, but not faint enough for Lily not to hear.

Lily pressed her lips together, the unexpected joy of his words giving her a fanciful hope that she affected him as much as he affected her. Her hope quickly faded, remembering their conversation about him getting married. To distract herself from her grave disappointment, she bent toward her foot. "Do you think my ankle is well soaked? I don't think I've felt my toes for a few minutes now."

Henry nodded and proceeded to unbutton his shirt to untie the cream-colored cravat from around his neck.

"What…what are you doing?" Lily didn't know whether to panic or stare in awe at the sun's rays shimmering off his smooth upper chest.

His gaze lifted, filtered through his thick lashes. "I need to wrap your ankle with something to keep the swelling down."

"Oh," Lily said, embarrassed her thoughts had become wayward and indecent. "I do think it's fine…ouch!" She winced and let out a wavering breath. It was still tender in places. "Do you suppose I've broken it?"

"No, it's just a sprain." He tied a knot at the top of her ankle, stood and reached out his hands. She hesitated, wondering when they had become unguarded and free, where nothing they did, caused disreputable thought or circumstance.

She surrendered to the moment, placing her palm in his, his grip strong and sturdy. He lifted her slight form and wrapped a steady arm around her waist. Against him, she felt alive, remembering all the reasons she had fallen in love with him in the first place.

"Do you think I should write and tell my father to send for me?" she asked as she set her injured foot onto the hard ground. It still hurt, but not as much as before.

He hesitated to answer, causing her to shift her gaze to his face.

"No." His voice reverberated with a thick and husky tone. In half a heartbeat, his lips crushed over hers. Lily braced herself, believing he meant to teach her a harsh lesson on improprieties. Only when his hand cupped the back of her head to bring her closer did she realize she had no energy to halt his punishment.

Barely able to stand, Lily leaned into his solid form,

drawing in the warm richness of his skin. With her hands braced on his shoulders, she lifted on the tiptoes of her good foot and raised the injured one behind her.

She savored the urgency of his kiss as her pulse hammered hard inside her veins. What they'd shared in the past did not come close to what she was sharing with him now. They had ascended from naïve innocence to desperation, to this moment where an intense hunger had both of them clinging to the next moment and each other.

Whether imprudently or foolishly, she mimicked the mingling dance of his tongue until a growl tore from his throat as he separated them, his gray eyes dark and stormy. Unable to stand on her own, she wrapped her fingers around the corded muscles of his arms. Oh, how she wished she had the ability to run away. How did one kiss have so much power over her? She knew it was because Henry was the one kissing her.

"You know no limits, do you, Miss Scott?" he said, his voice hushed and intolerant.

"You're the one who kissed me this time, Mr. Dalton," she snapped.

The muscle jumped in his jaw, and his chin lifted at an arrogant angle. "Yes, well, from this moment forward, we shall come to an agreement, madam; you will postpone showing Waverley your letter until I have quit Hadley, and I will refrain from kissing you again."

She mumbled her response. "I'm not sure who has the hardest task, you or me."

Having heard her, he lifted one dark eyebrow and stared down at her. "It is I, I assure you."

She tried to smile, only to swallow a lump of tears. When she started to hobble forward, Henry brought his arm across her hips and pulled her tight against his side.

"I'm confident you should be walking on it in a few days, but for now, you must take it easy. Just make sure to exercise it, to keep it from growing stiff."

She shook her head. "For someone who doesn't aspire to

be anything but a handsome and accommodating husband, you certainly know your way around the medical profession."

He nodded. "I make it a habit to dabble in a little of everything. One never knows when it will become useful or required," he added on an exhale.

Chapter Ten

Henry sat through the rest of the evening, unable to forget his special time with Lily at the waterfall. Before supper, he traveled back there, taking a dip in the frigid water to quell the heat of his rising and unfulfilled passions for her. For whatever reason, Henry had thought himself immune to her presence. Clearly, he had been wrong.

Of course, not long after his return, he learned, from Miss Appleton, naturally, that Waverley had been hinting of his growing attraction to Lily. His feelings were made evident in the dining parlor when Waverley took it upon himself to carry her to her seat.

Of course, she blushed and smiled, sending Henry into a

frenzy of emotions. *The devil!* He was the one who'd wrapped her blasted foot. Regardless, he could only sit and stare as she tilted her head with Waverley lowering his voice on purpose to bring her closer.

Henry's mood didn't improve when Miss Appleton dropped her hand under the table to accidentally brush her long fingers across his thigh. He believed she was trying harder to gain his attention. Unfortunately, she was doing nothing but turning his stomach.

Toward the end of the evening, he waited with patient fervor, for the servants to snuff out all the candles before traveling down the long corridor to Lily's room. He knew the exact door since she'd stayed in the bedchamber many times during her frequent visits. When he was fourteen, and she barely thirteen, they'd lie there together, the top of their heads touching. They never talked about growing older, somehow content to believe nothing would ever change.

At her door, he paused in the flickering darkness, his hand

raised, his heart thundering in his chest. Just as he was about to rap his knuckles across the thick wood, it opened. He blinked, finding Lily standing a foot away, her dark locks surrounding her face and her thick lashes fluttering like a kite in a windstorm.

"Mr. Dalton," she whispered, the candle in her hand placing intricate shadows over her flushed face. "I couldn't sleep."

He nodded. "I...uh...came to give you this." He withdrew the stick from under his arm. "It's to help you walk." He'd found it close to the waterfall, after an hour of searching.

She smiled until she glanced down to see another item that he held under his left arm. He'd thought about sneaking it into her room, but he would have missed the opportunity of watching her soft mouth open and close in surprise. "Did you think I wouldn't discover the author, Miss Scott?"

She shook her head. "I rather thought you wouldn't care enough to want to...discover her, sir."

She'd no sooner finished her sentence when a noise at the

end of the hallway propelled him across the threshold of her room. Without too much thought to the consequences, he whipped around and shut them both inside, alone. Lily remained quiet and unmoving behind him. A moment passed, her slight breathing becoming heavier with each heartbeat. When she finally spoke, her pleading voice trembled.

"You cannot stay."

He knew this more than anyone. However, he had no choice. He could face the scandal of leaving Lily's room or being caught inside with her, half-dressed, her lithe form intoxicating in the moonlight. He gambled with the later, strolling past her to stand a few feet away. Nothing had changed since the last time he was here, although it was still too dark to discern much of anything at this point. Still, he was able to see her bed, the mountain of covers tossed about like she was struggling to fall asleep. He smiled.

"I am curious," he said, placing the candle on her bedside table, "as to the unfortunate love affair of Miss Gravehart and Mr.

Mortimer. Are these people you know, or are they part of that whimsical mind of yours?"

She placed her candle next to his and limped toward him, using the cane he had brought her. "I believe, sir, that is none of your business."

His head tilted to see her better. "Defensive, are we?"

Her chest heaved in her thin nightgown, her curvaceous figure made more transparent by the flickering candles behind her. Henry's body tightened to taste her, touch her again.

"May I please have my book back, Mr. Dalton?" she asked, shuffling closer so that he could smell the sweet warmth of her skin.

"No."

"No? But...but it's not yours to keep."

"This is certainly true; however, I haven't finished reading it."

Her free hand fell to her waist, her fingers curling inside her palm. Henry recognized her frustration. Whether she loved

Waverley, whether she was about to become engaged to a man she cared nothing about, those facts didn't change the truth that he and Lily had a history together. She'd loved him first; of this, he was certain.

"Would it matter if I said that I never intended anyone to read them? They were for my eyes and my eyes only."

"What? Sort of like a diary?"

"Yes…no! Not like a diary."

"I see," he said, lifting his hand to caress the strands of her long, thick hair. "So, if you are Miss Gravehart, I am mad with curiosity to know the man you have disguised as Mr. Mortimer. Since I'm sure you wrote this prior to meeting Waverley, I'm wondering if poor Mortimer is someone else I know."

The revelation didn't surprise him. She was one and twenty with plenty of house parties to meet a gentleman who fancied more than two dances with her. For whatever reason, the thought of this man caused him more grief than her and his best friend.

In his silence, she sighed. "I am tired, sir. I wish only to hold those papers over a candle and toss them into the fire and go to bed."

His gaze shifted to her bed and then back to her. "Burning the compilation will not make your characters any less alive. They are now, forever, burned, you might say, into my memory."

Her fisted hand lifted, a finger pointed at his chest. "If you wish to flatter me—"

He inched forward, smashing her finger against his waistcoat and forcing her head to tip back. "I don't flatter, Miss Scott. I do, however, wish to know why you chose to make this Mortimer fellow immortal. Perhaps Waverley is not the man you love, but a mere distraction for someone whose rejection you have been unable to accept." He paused to let out a long, frustrated sigh. "Still, you have put a trance over my foolish friend even a blind man could see."

"I thought you didn't flatter, Mr. Dalton."

"I'm merely saying I see, along with everyone else here,

the way Waverley stares at you."

She dipped her head. "Now you are trying to embarrass me."

He crooked a finger under her chin, coaxing her mouth closer to his again. "That's not my intention at all. I'm merely stating that when you're around, Waverley, along with the other men at Hadley, are practically breaking their bloody necks to watch you brush a wayward wisp of hair from your green eyes."

She flinched, her cheeks reddening in the muted light of her room. "Now you're being ridiculous."

Henry realized she had no idea of the power of her presence. She had a way about her, without possessing the voluptuousness of Miss Appleton, who lured the opposite sex. Of course, he'd known Lily long before she'd grown into her curves. He'd known her when she gazed upon the world with such innocence and looked upon him with infatuation and misguided hope.

"Do you deny that it is your purpose to draw their

attention toward you, Miss Scott?"

"I deny it, entirely, sir. Despite what you think, I came to Hadley Manor to visit your sister. Jane, although older and too much of a romantic, always treats me well. You, on the other hand, are a boorish gentleman with opinions without facts."

He listened while Lily ranted breathlessly. Still, he was unable to keep his gaze from dropping to her lips as they puckered with indignation. He hadn't intended to kiss her on this night. He'd paid the physical price from the kiss he'd elicited from her earlier in the day. Besides, she'd proved herself too much of a flirt to be taken seriously. As well, there was the matter of his friend.

If Henry didn't think it might cause such a mess, he would call Waverley out, two pistols between them. Instead, he cut Lily's diatribe short with a pointed question: "Is it fiction, Miss Scott, that Mr. Waverley intends to ask for your hand?"

Chapter Eleven

Lily felt the blood rush from her face. "What?" She shook her head, wondering how any of this had happened. Of course, Lily thought, Jane must have suspected something since she'd postponed slipping the letter under Mr. Waverley's door.

"Miss Appleton informed me later this afternoon of the gentleman's intention of sending correspondence to your father. I don't know if he was bragging or just merely drunk. It could have been both."

Lily pulled away from Henry, her nerves rattled. She hobbled toward her bed and sank down on the firm mattress. "Per...perhaps, I should not have kissed him," she said absently.

"Yes, your letter would have been much more subtle, I

believe."

Lily drew back from his sarcastic tone. "Must you remind me on every occasion how, unlike your friend, your heart is unaffected by any gesture of fondness, whether it be a kiss or unguarded words of endearment?"

He stared at her, his gray eyes large and unblinking. Overwhelmed by the turn of events, she bent her head toward the floor. Now Jane would hate her, and she'd have to explain to her father why Mr. Waverley felt compelled to marry her after only two days in each other's company. She leaned over to wrap her arms around the bedpost, closing her eyes and resting her cheek against the cold beveled wood.

"I shall prove you wrong, madam."

Lily flipped her eyelids open to find Henry shrugging out of his waistcoat.

"What...what are you doing?"

He didn't answer, continuing to discard his cravat, and pull his white undershirt from his buckskin trousers. Lily had never seen him look so virile and dangerous, the intensity in his eyes giving her pulse a treacherous jolt.

He drew up close to her and halted. Too stunned to move or speak, she could only shake her head in astonishment.

"Do you wish me to go, Lily? If you do, say it now."

Words of protest stuck in her throat. She needed Henry to leave before they were caught, before society cast her out and her parents decided to never speak to her again. "We must not," she whispered trying to push him away. Her effort remained as weak as her heart.

The impropriety of her choice weighed heavily on her mind, until Henry reached down and grabbed her right wrist, sliding her palm under his shirt. Her hand pressed firm against the warmth of his smooth chest.

"Let me know, at any time, if I remain...unaffected," he said crushing his mouth to hers. He claimed her, once again, his kiss urgent and possessive. She lifted to meet him, to take what he offered, to give what he wanted.

"Lily," he breathed, coaxing her lips further apart. His tongue dove into the recess of her mouth and his free hand lifted to bring her closer. She started to float, the pulsating heat of his kiss lifting her with dizzying pleasure. Together, their hearts beat, uncaged and with such ferocity she struggled to catch her breath.

Empowered by his reaction to her, she imitated the delicious caress of his tongue. He groaned against her mouth, sending spirals of desire all the way to her midsection.

"Let me touch you," he begged. His words sounded husky and winded.

She nodded; her inexperience about what he meant giving him permission to grasp both sides of her arms and guide her further back on the bed. Like a panther, slow and cautious, he stretched out beside her.

Still half-dressed, he reached down to lift the hem of her nightgown. Cool air whipped across calf and upper thigh.

"Henry." She felt swept away by him, unsure which direction she needed to go to save her heart.

"Yes, it's me," he said, gliding his palm across her bare hip and maneuvering her onto her back. She trembled from the anticipation of his touch and gasped when his hand slid to press her legs further apart.

When his fingers parted her, she cried out, his mouth quick to cover hers in a kiss that was both primal and drugging. Delirious, her hips lifted and sank in rhythm to his light and caressing strokes. To deny him now would be like stopping her heart from beating.

Too lost to turn back, she chased the building pleasure at her core. What he was doing, the gentle sweeps across her most sensitive flesh, was driving her to a place of unsurpassed rapture. She thought the pleasure could not grow any stronger when he lowered his mouth and began teasing the nipple of her unbound breasts under the thin material of her nightgown. The heat from his kiss and the unrushed brush of his fingers pushed her higher to a blissful release. She was still floating in pulsing waves when his lips slid to her neck.

"You're mine, Lily, forever and always," he whispered in her left ear. Lily's eyelids flew open.

With her heart thundering, and his ramming hard against her palm, she wondered whether she'd imagined the words.

"From this moment forward, let there never be any doubt about what you do to me," he said, reaching down to withdraw her hand from where it lay against his chest. The separation stole the air from her lungs.

As if yanked from a dream, she sat up and thrust her nightgown over her shaky legs. Where she'd twisted her ankle, she felt the pulsing in every nerve.

"What…just happened?"

He blinked at her, his face devoid of either a smile or a frown. "You are a maid, and will remain so for your husband, whoever he may be."

A humiliating sob tore from her throat. She realized their future was set a long ago, without either one of them having a say one way or the other. Angrier than she'd ever seen him, he grabbed up his clothes, bowed, and left the room, neglecting to take the candle, or even dress properly.

Too stunned to move, Lily sat staring at the door.

But you are my husband. Shaken, she tried to recover her heart and soul from the place Henry had left them. After an hour of feeling sorry for herself, she forced herself up and wobbled straight to her writing desk.

Chapter Twelve

Henry lay awake for several hours; staring into the darkened shadows and feeling his world crush him on all sides. He wanted to return to London, to find a place to think about what he'd done and what he intended to do regarding Miss Lily Scott. For so long, he'd battled with the love he'd felt for her, had resigned himself to doing what his father wanted, had decided never to trust another woman again.

One thing he knew for sure, however; he'd never let Waverley marry her. Hell, Henry would much rather see his friend married to Jane than imagine the man ogling, touching, kissing, Lily the rest of his life. Henry had claimed her, although not fully. Even now, his heart ached to feel her hand against his chest, to smell her sweet scent lingering on his skin.

"God," he growled in agony, remembering her face as he brought her to pleasure. Then, he thought of how she'd gone to him so quickly. How did a woman who claimed to love another allow him to touch her in such a way? Was she a flirt or much worse? He closed his eyes, unable to comprehend such a thing. *She was his.*

Refusing to spend another moment at Hadley Manor, he picked up and quit the place before dawn. For the next two weeks, Henry kept his mind occupied, meeting with several acquaintances to learn whether there were any investments he might regard as highly profitable. He wanted to start working on buying the land he'd put off securing until now. Unfortunately, the more lucrative the investment, the more he stood to lose.

At his rented house in London, he labored by candlelight over Hadley's ledgers, discovering that its income compared with its total expenses did not leave a man with much choice other than to marry a wealthy woman. He only hoped the man he'd met regarding some risky investments might give him some good news. The prospect of him receiving six rather than four percent looked very well indeed. Still, he rubbed at his temples, unable to see himself tied to Miss Appleton or anyone like her if he yielded less than two percent. He loved only one woman.

His thoughts constant and draining, a knock sounded upon his door. When he glanced at the ticking mantel clock, he was shocked at the time. It was well past midnight. The knock grew louder and less patient.

"Wait," he called, lifting, and bringing the candle with him. He opened the door with a jerk, astonished to see Waverley on the other side.

"I've been charged, by your sister, to bring you this," the man said, stretching out his long arm to hand Henry a letter, folded and a little worn. Right away, Henry recognized the parchment paper and the careful creases. He also remembered the kiss that had rendered the letter from his pocket almost three weeks ago.

"How did you—,"

Waverley smiled, a tiny dimple on one side of his face making him even more attractive than Henry wanted to admit.

Henry thought about landing a stiff fist against his friend's cheek when Waverley thrust another letter in his direction. "I've also been asked to give this to you. Miss Scott left it behind with the first. You will notice it's written with the same cast of characters, namely you. I will be waiting in the carriage."

With a wink, Waverley bowed and backed away, stepping into the coach that had carried him all the way to Henry's front door. Determined to understand before giving himself hope over what his friend had said, Henry sat down at the writing table and unfolded the newer letter, dated two weeks ago.

Dear Jane,

It is with great sadness that I must leave Hadley Manor, at once. You see, I've been made aware of Mr. Waverley's intention to ask for my hand. I have no idea how this has happened. I should never have penned the letter you asked me to write him.

Dearest Jane, you must know, he was not the man for whom those

words were written.

I must confess, in my entire life, I've loved but one man. In

the garden, on the hottest day of August, you married us. Since

then, I've been unable to think or to dream of anyone else. I've

been cursed by his words, by his vow, and will remain so, forever

and always.

Henry exhaled, the words he'd just read, tilting his world.
How had he been so blind, so unable to see the truth of her
affection for him? He continued to read.

Please extend my apologies to Mr. Waverley. I believe I

must rush home to intercept any letter he has written to my father.

I should be married soon, to Mr. Gibbons. It's what's expected,

and I have told myself it will not be too dreadful, as long as I can

visit Hadley Manor and you.

Regards,

Lily

Henry stared at the fine words for a few moments before folding the letters and stuffing them both in his pocket. His body tight, his heart pounding, he rushed outside to join Waverley in the carriage.

"Should I ask how all this came about?"

Waverley shook his head. "I believe your sister would like to be the one to tell you."

Henry didn't argue and rode back to Hadley Manor, not a word spoken between him and his friend regarding Jane, or Lily.

Almost an hour later, after they had roused the servants, Henry marched straight to Jane's bedchamber, leaving Waverley in the parlor. Henry's nerves stretched taut to the point of snapping, he banged on her door, stepping back when it swung open.

"Hello, Henry." Of course, she was expecting him.

He reached into his jacket and pulled out the letter he had seized at Miss Scott's feet, the letter that had elicited a kiss, a touch, and weeks of physical agony. "I want you to explain this." His voice cracked as he waved the parchment in Jane's face.

"What in the devil is going on here?" Henry twisted around to find his father standing a few feet away. Beside him stood Henry's mother, a woman he had not seen in several years. He had to wonder if this 'reunion' was fate or another one of Jane's incorrigible schemes. Nevertheless, Henry thought his mother so altered that he almost didn't recognize her under her mobcap. Where he once remembered her bright eyes shining with youth, they now blinked with an underlying sadness he cared not to consider.

"My business does not concern you," he said to both of them. His father, tall and well built, eased out of his wife's hold.

"Very well, then. Do your business and meet me downstairs in fifteen minutes."

His father ambled away, leaving Henry's mother standing

in the middle of the darkened corridor, her gray eyes glistening with tears. She stepped forward, and Henry rotated away. He hated seeing her, hated remembering what he'd walked in on between her and another man.

"Henry." Her voice lifted to him, soft and trembling.

"No," he said, shaking his head.

"For God's sake, listen to me!" Her stern and desperate plea rotated him back around.

Chapter Thirteen

Henry's mother closed her tired eyes for a brief moment and folded her hands together as if in prayer.

"Before I married your father, there was someone else," she said, the words rushing forward and tumbling over themselves.

He nodded. "Yes, if you have not forgotten, after you were married, as well."

Her chin stiffened, and he was aware that she was about to educate him on her past, regardless of whether he wanted to hear the details or not.

"I was seventeen, and my father had just introduced me to his cousin, a wiry man who would inherit my father's property since I had no brothers. I was expected to marry Mr. Lawson, a man twenty years my senior who had already married and buried three wives. Needless to say, I was desperate not to become his fourth."

Henry stalked closer to where his mother stood, trembling. "How desperate?"

She dipped her head before bringing in a long inhale. "I was visiting my aunt and uncle in London when I met your father. We spent a few lovely afternoons together before the rumors of our innocent meetings reached my family. We were immediately separated. After some time, I forced myself to forget him."

Henry exhaled, seeing the parallels to his own life.

"Six months later, I met Frederick Brooks. He was amiable, but the son of a merchant who had nothing to offer but a meager living. Compared to what was arranged, Frederick's proposal seemed more than acceptable."

She paused, wiping at the tears streaming down her face. "We purchased rings with what little money Frederick had and agreed to travel to Gretna Green to get married."

Henry scoffed, "Nevertheless, unable to imagine a poor and uncomfortable living; you betrayed him first and later, the man you married?"

She brought in a stuttering breath. "Frederick never came for me. I waited a fortnight until a letter arrived, explaining how he'd changed his mind. He believed me in love with someone else. He told me to carry on with my life as if we'd never met."

Henry stared at his mother, unable to comprehend the pain of such a rejection. "So, who was the man I saw you with that day?"

Her head lifted. "Frederick's brother. He'd come to tell me that Frederick had…died, unmarried, and wearing the ring I was to have given him at Gretna Green. A letter was left with instructions to return the ring to me upon his death."

Henry's mouth fell in disbelief at his mother's words. When his gaze shifted to his sister, he found her unmoving and her blue eyes wide and unblinking. Now, she knew the truth of why he'd chosen to stay away so long.

His mother took a cautious step closer to him. "Frederick was right, Henry. I was in love with someone else: your father. When we were separated, I thought his absence meant he'd chosen to forget me, as well. I was wrong. Despite his parents' hesitation, he was determined to marry me."

Henry was unable to move forward or utter one word for a full minute. "Why didn't you say something? Why didn't you stop me from drawing the worst conclusion?"

She sent him a weak smile. "You were so angry with me. Whenever I tried to talk to you, you'd walk away. I even tried writing you letters, and they all came back, unopened."

In the muted light, he shifted closer and wrapped his arms around his mother's soft and comforting form. "I…I never imagined," he whispered.

She reached up and touched his face, pulling slightly away from him. "Your father even tried talking to you, but you shut him out, too. For different reasons, I suppose."

Henry nodded. He'd stopped talking to his father soon after he'd changed his future to not include Lily.

"I have watched you, and her grow together and apart. You must find a way to be with her, Henry."

He knew his mother spoke of Lily. However, Henry still had to reconcile his father to his decision to marry a woman who might place Hadley at the mercy of creditors. Of course, he'd just learned that each of his parents had made their own choices, and they had done well for the decisions they had made. For himself, Henry wanted Lily. She might deserve better than him, but she was his, and he was hers, forever and always.

His thoughts heavy, he stalked downstairs and met his father, finding the man talking to Waverley as if they were the oldest of friends. They both glanced up, his father standing and motioning for him to have a seat. Henry shook his head, prepared to take his father's latest advice standing up.

Too warm for a fire, the housekeeper had placed four candles on the mantelpiece to illuminate the room into iridescent shadows.

"Are we all on speaking terms, again?" his father asked.

Henry nodded, although he was not up to hearing the man lecture him again on why Lily was not the right choice.

"Very well. I will not waste your time. Although you have inherited your mother's emotional heart, I want to believe you have inherited my common sense. With that said, it is your choice to make, so make it well. And if you must follow your heart, I would suggest contacting a Mr. Braxton in London. He knows of a few ventures or investments where you could see a return of up to four percent. Then, you and Miss Scott might find both love and comfort at your disposal."

Henry smiled at his father, having already met with the man several times. "What has made you change your mind?"

It took the elder Mr. Dalton a few moments to give his son an answer. "Your mother." He brought in a deep breath and said nothing more regarding their past. "I won't regret separating you and Miss Scott."

"You believe Miss Scott would have been a mistake?"

His father shook his head. "You were both so very young: she too impressionable and you too impulsive. I gave you an alternative—,"

"You gave me an ultimatum," Henry reminded him, his temper rising.

"I gave you a chance to step back and make the right decision. You are a man now with experience and vision."

It was Henry's turn to shake his head. "I could have lost her!"

"You know your sister and your mother would not have let that happen. I was quite outnumbered when it came to her."

Henry reconciled with his father's meddling and started to step away when a question propelled him back around. "I am curious. How did you know so much of my feelings toward Lily back then?"

His father sent him a sly smile. "Your aunt, though odd, is very observant and has learned to sleep with one eye open. Why else is she allowed to chaperone your most capricious sister?"

"Why indeed?" Henry said before glancing over to send Waverley a respectable nod. His friend smiled, seeming content to finish his conversation with Henry's father.

With his energy elevated to such heights, Henry took the stairs two at a time. He found Jane's door open and her settled upon the window seat, her knees drawn to her chin.

He softened his steps across the thin rugs in front of her bed and sank beside her, waiting for an explanation.

"I'm astonished by Mother's confession. Are you?" his sister asked.

He kept the answer to himself for a few silent moments. "I am more relieved by it than anything."

Jane appeared to be waiting for further explanation, but when it became apparent that he wasn't going to add anything else, she brought in a loud breath. "Believe it or not, the letter was not my idea, but rather, your friend's," she said after a long moment of silence.

Henry drew back, surprised. "Waverley?"

Jane nodded. "He came to me two months ago, asking questions about a woman you had mentioned several times, mostly in a state of drunkenness."

"Lily," Henry breathed. He knew she'd taken over his heart. He just didn't realize she'd invaded his mind, as well.

"So, we came up with a way to bring you and Lily together to settle your feelings for one another somehow. Although I have witnessed her love for you grow for more than seven years, you did everything in your power to extinguish it."

He closed his eyes for a brief moment. Yes, he'd pushed Lily away with words and with time. Now he wondered whether his actions were both unforgivable and irreparable. What if he'd lost her? "I was a pompous fool," he admitted, remembering the name Lily had called him. "So, you made her write a letter to me?"

"I encouraged her to write a letter to the man who held her heart, disguising it as a note that I would give to Mr. Waverley. It was to be a confession, of sorts." She paused to stifle a giggle. "Every step of the way was planned."

He didn't think it all so humorous. "Then you stole her plays?" Henry asked. He was disappointed Jane would stoop so low to bring him and Lily together.

"No, that was all Miss Appleton's doing, with Mr. Waverley finding the disingenuous endeavor advantageous. And, you must admit, your friend made you jealous enough. That kiss she gave him was just the right amount of ammunition to feign being in love with her, although I can't help but think that he enjoyed every minute of it."

Henry drew his hand down the length of his face. "Did you intend to sprain her ankle, too?"

His sister sent him a disgusted look. "No, of course not! Apparently, Mr. Waverley is chivalrous beyond comprehension and saw himself saving poor Lily from a swan attack. What happened next was a series of events that could only be explained by an intervention of fate."

Henry scoffed but didn't deny some truth to her words, which brought him full circle to his friend's intentions toward his sister. "Jane—"

"No, I have not lost my heart to Mr. Waverley. However, I must admit, if you promise not to shoot him, he does fascinate me."

Henry smiled. "I will not make any such promise." Now, too eager to linger much longer, he lifted from his seat, bending down to place an affectionate kiss upon her head.

"What are you to do now?" she asked, grasping his hand.

"Pray I'm not too late," he said.

Chapter Fourteen

Lily sat at her writing desk in the early morning light, laboring over a scene she'd dreamed about in the middle of the night. There was a new character, a Mr. Winston, who had challenged Mr. Mortimer to a duel. Her thoughts moving faster than the quill and the ink, Lily worked valiantly to write down the number of paces between the men and the type of pistol both held in their right hands.

"Lily, dear?"

Lily jumped at her mother's quiet voice and soft knock.

"What is it, Mama?"

"Your father is asking for you in his study."

Lily dropped her shoulders and then her quill. Mr.

Mortimer's fate would have to wait, she supposed. For now, Lily

needed to explain to her father, for the tenth time that week, why

she didn't wish to marry Mr. Gibbons, or anyone else, for that

matter. This was the turn of the nineteenth century, and surely,

she could find a respectable occupation that might earn her a

comfortable living. Perhaps she could sell one of her plays.

With another speech in her head, she opened her door and

found her mother waiting for her outside her room.

She was a short woman with a round face and light-green

eyes. Timid and affectionate, she grasped Lily's arm and walked

with her down a flight of stairs to the closed door of her father's

study. When Lily turned to smile at her mother, she noticed a tear

rolling down the woman's glistening cheek.

Lily's heart careened against her ribcage, suddenly

anxious regarding her father's summons and whatever was

making her mother forlorn enough to elicit tears. "What—"

The doorknob rattled, and the door opened with her father

standing on the other side. He was dressed in his finest attire, his lips raised in a rare smile. Lily glanced from one parent to another, unable to predict what the next few minutes held for her. Her father had every right to deny her what she wanted for the good of the family. Of course, what she truly wanted and could never have was Henry Dalton. It was all very well. It was best she forget about him…well unless his character was shot at by his best friend, Mr. Winston.

"You wished to see me, Papa?" she said, her throat tightening, despite her hardened thoughts.

"Yes," he said, tilting his head down, so his brown eyes peered over his spectacles. "Come and sit with me next to the window. It is a glorious morning."

Lily untangled herself from her mother's hold and left her standing in the doorway to take a seat in an apple-green and white striped settee. It was indeed, a glorious morning, the grays and blues of dawn yet to dissolve into the heat of the sun.

"It does a father well," Mr. Scott began, "to know that he no longer has to worry about the welfare of his youngest child."

Lily closed her eyes and pressed her lips together, afraid if she didn't, he might glance over at her and see them quiver. Oh, she didn't want to think about having to marry Mr. Gibbons. Not only did she not love him, but she'd also come to realize he was a man who would leave her for weeks at a time without a care to her feelings.

"So, it gives me great pleasure to give you this."

Lily opened her eyes to find a letter waiting for her on her lap. "Who—"

Her father shook his head. "You will see."

Please don't be from Mr. Waverley. Please don't be from Mr. Waverley. With trembling hands, Lily opened the small folded paper and let her jaw drop to her chest.

Mr. Scott,

It has been brought to my attention your daughter is not, in fact, free to marry as I was led to believe. I would call this a just impediment. As may be expected, I wish not to pursue your daughter any further.

    Regards,

    Mr. Gibbons

Lily could not imagine who had brought this *impediment* to Mr. Gibbons' attention. Regarding Henry, there were too many to mention. Still, she couldn't guess why he'd gone to such trouble to tell the man. After all, Henry had made it quite clear that he didn't intend to pursue her either. Needless to say, he also had made it clear he didn't even like her very much.

As a blush of humiliation began to rise from her midsection into her cheeks, she glanced toward her father.

"I was shocked, to say the least," Mr. Scott said, gently taking the parchment out of her hand. "After all, what on earth could Mr. Gibbons mean?"

Lily shook her head, the heat from her rising blush beginning to dampen her temples.

"Then I received this letter."

Again, Lily glanced down to find another folded letter in her lap. Her fingers trembled worse this time, and her heart thundered from what her father might have discovered. Her throat so constricted with emotion, she could do nothing but unfold the correspondence.

Dear Mr. Scott,

I am ashamed to learn that I may have caused the unhappiness of a dear friend. You see, sir, seven years ago, I married your daughter to my brother, Henry Dalton, an act born of boredom and romantic circumstance. As innocent as it was, my brother insists, without delay, that he and your daughter come to a resolution regarding the matter.

Regards,

Miss Jane Dalton

Lily blinked, her vision blurred by tears and frustration. When she finally folded up the letter and handed it back to her father, she felt as if her world had turned black and gray. Resolution? Did Henry think their act of marriage, though immature and impulsive, was so disgusting that he needed a resolution?

Lily felt her eyebrows furrow together, and her fingers curl into a fist at her side. Who was Jane or Henry to undo seven years of her life? Both angry and disappointed, she faced her father. Of course, he was smiling. Although Mr. Scott was sometimes unrelenting and serious, he did love a good laugh on occasion.

"Then there is the matter of this letter," her father said, replacing the note Lily had just read with another shorter one. She inhaled and let out a quiet breath. Who was left to write?

Dear Mr. Scott,

I know this is unprecedented; however, I would like a visit with you to discuss my intention of marrying your daughter. I await your answer in your parlor.

Lily's heart stopped before slamming hard into her ribcage. She searched for a signature, only to find there wasn't one. But it had to be from Mr. Waverley. He was the only gentleman who appeared to want her for a wife. *Dear God.* Although she liked him very much, she couldn't see destroying Jane's heart in the process of settling for a comfortable marriage.

"It is most extraordinary, is it not?" her father asked.

Lily sat up straighter. "Yes, but I can't marry the man who wrote you this letter," she whispered, a stray tear slipping past her eyelashes to fall onto her cheek.

Her father, as affectionate as her mother, placed an arm around her shoulder. "Why not?"

Lily, for once in her adult life, needed to tell the truth to her parents, as well as to herself. "Because I'm in love with Mr. Henry Dalton, and I cannot, under any circumstance, bind myself to any man but him." She blew out a breath as her father sat staring, unblinking, in her direction. Whether Henry loved her, no longer mattered.

When enough time had passed, her father nodded and stood. "In that case, I suppose I cannot delay my answer to the gentleman any longer."

Lily opened her mouth to ask his meaning, only to receive a pat on her right cheek. After the doors had closed, she sat for a moment. "Oh, this is a complete and utter disaster," Lily whispered, contemplating having to disappoint everyone. If her father meant to marry her to Mr. Waverley without delay, to keep the man from learning of her heart affair with Mr. Dalton, she realized she was in the same situation as before. No. That would not do.

Perhaps if she brought Jane back here, Mr. Waverley might be convinced to change his mind about whom he loved. She also believed it was time to confront Henry about her feelings for him. She only prayed he wouldn't stand and laugh at her when she did.

More desperate than logical, Lily rushed from the room

and outside, hurrying past the black carriage in front of the house and toward the gig her mother always wanted ready for her early morning rides.

Without stopping to let anyone know, Lily climbed onto the light, two-wheeled vehicle and snapped the reins, spurring the gelding into motion.

She supposed she'd drawn up within a mile of Hadley Manor when she heard the pounding of horse hooves behind her. The mist of the morning had yet to disappear when there was already another traveler, an impatient one, to be sure, traveling on the same road with her.

Unwilling to be trampled on, Lily pulled left on the reins and guided the horse to the edge of the narrow road. She'd wait until the rider passed by her. Only, the galloping horse skidded to a stop behind her carriage, forcing her to spin around to see why.

Her heart lurched forward as she sat staring into a set of steel-gray eyes. "Mr. Dalton?"

Chapter Fifteen

"Miss Scott," he said, tipping his head in her direction. A short, loud exhalation later, he leaned forward and slid to the ground, his Hessian boots landing with a thud on the dry road. In stunned silence, Lily watched as he tied his horse to the back of the carriage. No, not his horse, but her father's horse. But how—

"We need to talk, Miss Scott."

"Yes, I've become very aware of that, sir. Were you in such a hurry to bring about our *resolution* that you needed to run me down?"

He sent her a half-cocked smile. She huffed out a frustrated sigh and turned away until he climbed onto the gig and gently transferred the reins out of her hands. Now, confronted with his presence, she didn't think her heart could handle confessing her true feelings. What if he glanced down his straight nose at her and scoffed at such a notion?

"Yes," he said and changed the subject slightly. "I would like to know if you were headed in the direction of Hadley Manor?" he asked.

"I…yes. I need to speak with your sister about an urgent matter."

"Which reminds me," he said, pausing to lift a letter from inside his jacket. "Would you care to explain this?"

Lily's stomach dropped to her bent knees. She stared at the letter he held in his left hand, knowing it was the one that had slipped out of her sleeve so many nights ago. She wasn't prepared to tell him the truth. She'd had no time to rehearse her words. "Since I'm not sure how you came to possess the item, again, no, sir. I'd rather not."

As Henry spurred the gelding forward, Lily sat staring, astonished and mortified, wondering if he knew what she and

Jane had done.

"I don't think I'm used to you staying so quiet. It's a bit unnerving."

She scoffed, unsure whether he was insulting her or merely paying her a compliment. "Perhaps you should ask Jane about the letter."

"I have and now it's your turn, Miss Scott. I shall ask you a question, and you will give me a 'yes' or 'no' answer."

Too weary to assume anything about his and Jane's conversation, Lily braced her hands on the seat and awaited his inquisition. She prayed she could delay her answers long enough to reach Hadley Manor.

"First question: Are you in love with the man to whom you wrote the letter?"

Lily dropped her shoulders. The truth would not hurt her here. "Yes, Mr. Dalton. Were my words not clear enough?"

He chuckled, causing her to turn toward him once again. He cleared his throat and continued. "Next question: Have you allowed this man to kiss you?"

Lily smashed her lips together, content to let the inquiry go without an answer.

"I asked, madam if you allowed the man you love to kiss you."

"I heard you, sir, and yes," Lily said, so angry she believed she had as little control over her tongue as she had over her emotions. "I allowed him to kiss me; however, do not imagine it was because I was weak or a flirt. You are so insensitive; you wouldn't understand what it's like to be near someone, to feel so connected and in love with them that every breath you take is part theirs, part your own." The words flew out before she could stop them, causing Henry to pull back on the leather straps, jerking the carriage to an abrupt stop.

Lily clung to her seat with her heart pounding from both her confession and the anticipation of what he planned to do. By now, she should have been used to them teetering on the edge of scandal. Still, she glanced back, praying no one was traveling this early to start the rumor of her ruin. Of course, the rumor was most likely already circulating, what with her intended intercepting the wedding banns, and poor Mr. Waverley still standing in her father's parlor, probably assuming she was in the next room and not off, unchaperoned, with his friend.

"And he knows this?" Henry asked, drawing closer. "He knows that every breath you take while in his company is part his?"

She stilled her nerves and lifted her chin higher. "No."

"Why?"

Immersed in Henry's company and his inquisition, she hadn't paid any attention to where they were going. Nothing seemed at all familiar. She twisted in one direction and then the next. "Where…are we?"

"You will answer my question first."

"What you asked, was not a 'yes' or 'no' question. Therefore, I do not feel obligated to answer it," she said, braving his wrath with an insolent response.

"Very well, Miss Scott."

Lily had yet to congratulate herself on her victory when he stepped down from the carriage, grasped her bare hand, and hauled her to the ground beside him.

"Why are you doing this?"

He didn't answer, pulling her toward a curtain of trees. She wasn't afraid of where he was taking her, only afraid he might leave her, alone.

Inside the forest walls, they crunched over fallen limbs, weaved through thick branches, and ducked under twisted logs. The air was cooler and lighter here. Lily inhaled, bringing in the richness of the damp earth and thick foliage.

"Getting me lost will not make me answer any more of your questions, Mr. Dalton."

His reply was a mere grunt. A moment later, Lily heard the rush of falling water. In a blink, he hauled her through a vertical crack in a mammoth moss-covered rock.

When he halted, and let go of her hand, it took her a

moment to realize she stood between a rushing waterfall and a wall of wet stone. The coolness of the alcove brushed across her heated skin.

"Now, I will ask you again, Miss Scott. Why?" His voice lifted over the roar of the rushing water.

Lily opened and closed her mouth several times before choosing to ask her questions. "And why is it so important for you to know who I love? A few weeks ago, you didn't even remember my name."

He stalked closer; looking every bit as feral as the panther she compared him to a few weeks ago. Since the room behind the waterfall didn't afford much movement, she had no choice but to stay in place. By now, the dense mist had soaked clear to their skin. With his hair darkened and matted to his face, she fought the urge to reach up and touch him.

"You are wrong, Miss Scott. I knew your name. I just didn't want to be reminded of it."

She blanched, stabbed by his words. Whether she meant to

make a full confession or not, she lashed out. "You...you are a hateful man, and I can hardly believe I allowed myself to remain so ardently in love with you for the last seven years of my life!"

****

Henry grasped Lily by her waist and hauled her hard against him. She struggled, her sweet breath sweeping across his wet face, stirring his need for her even deeper. Since last night, he'd thought of little else but having her confess her true feelings. For years, he'd hidden behind his anger while she'd hidden behind her quill.

Now, with her white empire dress clinging to her curvy body, he brought up his hand to cup one side of her face. She was the loveliest creature he'd ever seen, even with her evergreen eyes glistening with unsuppressed anger.

"Have you thought to ask me why?" he said, his gaze narrowing. "Have you wondered, after so many years in each other's company, I chose to forget you?"

She stilled.

"Good. I have your attention." He paused to inhale. "There was a time I had planned our future together, every moment, every day. I was going to purchase more land for Hadley, and you were going to...*remain* my wife."

She opened her mouth several times, seeming to struggle with what to say. "So, so...what happened?"

"I learned what it meant to be the only son of a prominent English family. I also saw things I was not mature enough to question. The combination threw us apart, and I believed I could put you out of my heart as quickly as I put you out of my mind."

"It did not come so quickly for me," she murmured.

"Believe me; I have suffered. I suffered until I was so overwrought with disappointment; I could not bear to recall your memory. Only, I came to Hadley Manor, and with one look in your direction, I found my breath stolen."

Her quietness unsettled him. He lowered his forehead to hers and closed his eyes. "I had it wrong seven years ago. You didn't become mine; I became yours. The *resolution* my sister spoke of in her letter, is that we never find ourselves separated from each other again."

He felt her shoulders drop, felt the erratic beating of her heart as he held her close. She seemed to remember why she was traveling to Hadley in the first place and pushed away from him. "No. Mr. Waverley has informed my father of his wish of marrying me. He wrote a note, detailing his intentions. He's there, talking to him as we speak. It's too late!"

Henry smiled and caressed her soft, wet cheek with his thumb. "I'm afraid there is much to discuss regarding Waverley and my sister. However, for now, I will say that I arrived with him at your home over an hour ago. The note to which you refer was from me, not my friend."

When her mouth opened in surprise, he bent to kiss her, drinking the sweet dew from her wet lips. He pulled away slightly to whisper his thoughts. "I love you, Lillian Elizabeth Scott. Will you marry me, again?"

She brought her hands up to cup his face, tears streaming

down her cheeks. "Yes." She hiccupped the word. She smiled until her eyebrows narrowed over her misty eyes. "But, what of your dreams? Certainly, my dowry is not enough for us to live well?"

He smiled. "Then I shall become a doctor."

She harrumphed, seeming to remember his gruff bedside manner when she'd sprained her ankle. "I believe we should think of something else?" she teased.

He bent to lay soft kisses across her forehead. "We shall sell one of your plays. When I showed your compilation to a theatrical friend of mine in London, he offered one hundred and fifty pounds, plus royalties, for Mr. Mortimer and Miss Gravehart."

Her eyebrows furrowed. "How—"

"Why do you think it took me so long to give them back to you?"

Her eyes widened. "Oh."

"Although the edited version we performed might bring in a higher price," he taunted her, still remembering the crack of the slap as her palm connected with his face.

Her gaze dipped to his chest. "Between then and now, I…might have added a duel."

He threw back his head and laughed. When he'd sobered from his mirth, he drew her closer. "Well, of course, you did, my love."

Then, he paused, pulling away slightly to whisper his thoughts. "I wish I did not have to wait until our wedding day to touch you again."

Her hands lifted to his water-laden waistcoat, her words whispering back to him. "If I recall correctly, Mr. Dalton, we *are* married."

Henry needed no other prompting. Spurred by a fervor he could no longer control, he crushed his mouth to hers. She reached between them, her fingers fumbling for his buttons, starting with his waistcoat and then his shirt.

He claimed her lips with unbridled possession, his body tightening and his heart thundering so loudly, it drowned out the crash of the waterfall. She melted into him as his tongue stroked the inside of her delicious mouth.

He kissed her as he unfastened an ungodly amount of strings and maneuvered her to where a bed of moss lay covering the floor at the falls edge. Her lush, naked body slid beneath his, her arms lifting to wrap around his neck to pull him closer.

God, how many nights had he dreamed of this moment, of making her truly his? *Too many.*

His hands roamed over her velvety waist and up to the curve of her left breast. He glided his thumb over a dusky pink nipple until she moaned and her hips arched into his aching and swollen shaft. The tormenting connection shot fire through his veins, leaving him breathless and shaking.

"Lily," he whispered, skimming his lips across her rounded cheek to the satiny skin below her ear. He loved touching her. More than this, he loved tasting her. Sweet and exotic, he glided his mouth to the peak of one breast.

She was the paradise he'd been chasing, the rapture he'd been hoping to find. Only, she had been right in front of him the entire time. No longer able to keep them apart, he shifted above her and wrapped his arms around her, cradling her head with one hand. He felt her tremble, felt her lift to accept him. He held her tighter, gazing into her brilliant face before burying himself inside her.

Lily tensed and then held her breath, digging her short finger nails into Henry's bare shoulder. She had not prepared herself for the pain or the shock of their union. "Henry," she gasped.

She shook beneath him. Without breaking their connection, he rested his forehead on hers. It took him a moment to steady his voice, his tone sounding low and husky. "Hold on to me," he whispered, gently cupping her jaw, and covering her mouth with the most tender of kisses.

The need for him to fill her overpowered Lily's fear and discomfort. Like he instructed, she tightened her grip and held on until his rhythmic movements began to rouse the familiar ache he'd introduced her to a few weeks before. This time, the fervent desire to draw him closer and deeper increased the tension building inside her. She let herself relax and tilted her head back as the enveloping intensity grew with exquisite madness.

Henry had imagined this moment a thousand times through the years. However, he'd never dreamed how tightly and exquisitely perfect she would mold around him. "Lily," he rasped, trying to keep from losing himself inside her so soon.

He retreated from her only to have her arch upward, a cry of disappointment on her lips. Unable to hold back, he gathered her against him before driving hard inside her. He buried his mouth against her neck, riding his release as it came fast and forceful. She clung to him as they both convulsed and exploded on an overpowering wave of surrender. He spilled himself inside her, each uncontrollable spasm shuddering through him like a lightning bolt.

Lily's pulse throbbed up and down her weary body. Reluctantly, she floated down from the spiraled heights to which he'd taken her. She wanted to stay like this forever with him and with the mist of the waterfall cooling their glistening bodies.

"It feels like a dream," she said, opening her eyelids to gaze up at him. "A dream I never want to wake from."

He smiled down at her. He was braced on his elbows while his fingers smoothed the damp tendrils from her face.

"Yes." Henry had wanted her to say this, to not regret one moment between them. At last, the world he thought had collapsed upon itself, fell, wonderfully into place.

The End

Book 2

The Matchmaker's Surrender

Miss Jane Dalton, one of London's most successful matchmakers, would rather bring couples together than choose a gentleman for herself. In fact, she could not think of anything more frightening than falling in love. Fate, however, disrupts her plans to remain a single matchmaker when Mr. Nicholas Waverley, her brother's best friend, is forced to kidnap her after she becomes entangled in an assassin's web.

Brought together under dangerous circumstances, Jane realizes her true feelings for Nicholas. In the end, however, is her love for him worth the fall?

Releasing May 20, 2019

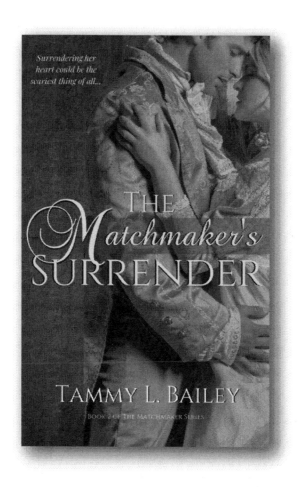

The Matchmaker's Surrender

Chapter One

England 1817

"I pronounce that they be man and wife..."

Miss Jane Dalton glanced around the quaint church into the sea of muslin Empire gowns and black tailcoats and smiled.

It had turned out to be a perfect day, with the sun's light filtering in through the Gothic tracery windows. The mahogany pews were filled with people ready to witness her brother and best friend's official wedding. For Henry and Lily, however, their happily-ever-after had not come easily.

Since officiating a fake wedding ceremony between Lily and Henry when they were all very young, Jane always imagined them together. One might say it was the moment that began her matchmaking endeavors. With numerous parties and gatherings, she'd succeeded in bringing together over a dozen couples. To date, she'd attended most of their weddings.

This wedding was her favorite by far. She supposed she could not have done it without the help of Henry's best friend, Mr. Waverley. By nudging fate, they had both colluded on one of the most romantic reunions in recent history.

"When will it be your turn?"

Jane glanced to find Lily and Henry walking down the aisle and the local busybody, Mrs. Abram, tugging at her elbow. Jane's mother, who stood up to leave behind the newly married couple, turned back to send Jane a regretful glance. Her father, on the other hand, tried to linger to catch her answer, but was dragged away by Mrs. Dalton. The other witness to Mrs. Abram question was none other than Mr. Waverley himself, who stood a few feet away.

At a loss for words, Jane brushed a wisp of light brown hair from her eyes and forced a smile. What could she say? *The thought of falling in love gives me the vapors?* Not that she'd ever had her heart broken. If she had, she might understand her anxiety more. No, her aversion to falling in love was more existential. She believed it was better to have never loved than to have loved and lost. In her opinion, it was what made her a good matchmaker. Her heart was pure, unscarred, and unbroken. With her entire being, she meant to keep it that way.

Besides, the only gentleman with whom she'd had any interesting conversation these last eight months was Mr. Waverley.

Bothered by her thoughts, she stole a glance in his direction and swallowed a sigh. Dressed in a pair of tan breeches, a black tailcoat, and gold waistcoat, he stood as tall as she remembered. Not towering, but the perfect height for a dance partner. She did remember him being thinner than Henry, but today, his shoulders appeared broader and more muscular.

His dark blond hair had grown longer since they'd last spoken as well, so it touched the collar of his waistcoat. The one thing that hadn't changed was his glinting blue eyes.

Although he was very handsome, he seemed to exude a placatory personality that did not appeal to Jane in any way. She supposed when a man possessed both handsomeness and wealth, he wasn't required to work on doing more than bowing, smiling, and sometimes flirting to gain the affection of her fairer sex. At least, that is what she told herself.

As if reading her mind, Mr. Waverley turned and sent her a slight bow and a breathtaking smile. Jane's heart bounced unexpectedly. Her quick intake of breath was not lost on him. His smile deepened, causing the dimple on his right cheek to become more pronounced. *Oh dear.*

She glanced away and squeezed her eyes closed for a brief moment. She didn't want to give

Nicholas the impression she was trying to gain his

attention.

"Shall we?"

Jane shifted her gaze back to him and then around the church to find it almost empty. She supposed she'd hesitated too long when Mr. Waverley cleared his throat and presented her with an amused grin. "I'm not known to bite, Miss Dalton, if that's your concern."

She clicked her tongue and pressed her gloved palm against his forearm.

"But you are certainly known for other things," she mumbled, recalling the rumors of his sometimes immoral behavior.

When he cocked his head and arched an eyebrow, she wished she'd kept her comment to herself. Then his strong muscles flexed under her hand, surprising her. For as long as she'd known him, she'd never thought of him as strong or even dominant. Now, she wondered if he possessed some other attractive feature that might cause her to blush or falter her step?

Anxious of what she might discover, she withdrew her hand and paused just outside the open doorway. "I…believe, I should go and assist Lily on…something."

Jane shifted away when Mr. Waverley's fingertips grasped hers. The sudden and scandalous intimacy sent a ripple of excitement through her. "Sir, I—"

"I'm determined to have a ball soon. I would like very much if you could attend," he leaned down to say into her ear, the warmth of his touch seeping through the thin fabric of her glove. She tried to pull away, to put some distance between herself and these rather abrupt and confusing feelings.

Whether it was tomorrow or a year from now, she didn't want him to believe she thought more of him than as a friend. Alternatively, she didn't want to think of him as more than a friend.

"That would be lovely," she found herself saying after a long pause.

He smiled, the brilliant color in his blue eyes holding her

hostage for a second or two. Had they always been so blue?

"Mr. Waverley," she said, curtsying.

"Miss Dalton," he replied, sending her a quick bow. When he nodded a farewell, Jane stifled a sense of disappointment. When he rotated toward a crowd of mothers and blushing daughters, she suppressed a wave of jealousy.

"Ridiculous flirt," she mumbled before striding away at a brisk pace. She followed the wedding party down the dirt path that led to Hadley Manor. It was a short stroll, but too long to mull over her feelings. To occupy her mind on anything or anyone other than Mr. Waverley, she tried to concentrate on the gregarious chattering of a few sparrows nearby. Today, their noisy songs only seemed to mock her.

Flustered, she descended the stone steps near the garden in the back of the house. She searched for Lily, finding her friend standing near a water fountain. Jane believed her to be the loveliest of brides. Her beige Empire dress accentuated her flowing dark hair, olive complexion, and emerald green eyes.

Out of breath, Jane reached her friend.

"What's the matter, Jane?" Lily asked. "You're blushing. Who has you so ruffled?"

Jane brought her hands to her face. "It's from the exercise, surely you must see that," she replied, mortified Lily might guess her tangled thoughts regarding Mr. Waverley.

A slow smile lifted the corner of Lily's mouth. "Oh, Jane. It's Mr. Waverley. You like him!"

"No! Goodness, no," Jane answered, perhaps with a little too much emphasis. She cleared her throat and swatted a piece of hair from her face. "Mr. Waverley, indeed. Why, I've...never met a more...a more—" "Handsome?"

Jane clicked her tongue. "Unpretentious man," she corrected her friend.

Lily drew back, and they both twisted in Mr. Waverley's direction. He stood speaking to several ladies, a few of them waving their fans as if performing some mating ritual.

"Well, Jane, they certainly don't think your Mr. Waverley

is…unpretentious."

"Oh, stop it, Lily," Jane scolded, "He's not *my* Mr. Waverley." Of course, Jane couldn't help but stare after him and his group of admirers. She remembered how her brother often spoke about Mr. Waverley's libertine ways. She didn't doubt he could be quite devilish; however, Jane wondered, as she gazed upon him now, if her brother had exaggerated his friend's indiscretions.

Unfortunately, he seemed to sense them looking and shifted his eyes squarely to Jane's.

He smiled and bowed.

Embarrassed she'd been caught staring at him, Jane twirled, showing him her back. "He does seem to like the attention, doesn't he?" she said, trying to keep the bite out of her tone.

"Perhaps not as much as you find it vexing," Lily giggled.

"You're wrong. I don't like Mr. Waverley in the least. I believe he is so accommodating and unassuming; I almost wish he would say or do something so shocking, it would make me faint straight away."

Lily smashed her lips together, but the shudder in her slight shoulders told Jane she was trying not to give in to a fit of laughter. Jane scoffed and started to walk away when her friend grasped her hand and hauled her back in front of her.

"You would never let me get away with such a comment. Now, what sort of thing would you wish Mr. Waverley to do, Jane?" I must know."

Jane opened and closed her mouth a few times before realizing the scandalizing truth. For several months, her mind had kept wandering back to the play he and Lily had performed at the party months before. It was the same play that had fanned her curiosity about Mr. Waverley's

lips.

"What? What is it?" Lily prodded, bending closer.

"Who are we discussing so huddled close together?"

Other books by this Author

A Mistress for Penndrake (Historical Romance)

The Marquess of Wesley, Earl of Chelmsford, is out for blood. For a year, Lord Wesley has tried to undo the devastation his father left to Penndrake, their ancestral home, only to discover the man gambled it away right before his death. Now Wesley is being blackmailed by the new owner into marrying a woman he's never met in order to get it back. But his intentions are less than honorable...

At one and twenty, Miss Kate Holden intends to become a governess, having sworn off all men years ago. However, her plans are halted when she receives a daunting letter from her cousin about a Lord Wesley. Ignorant of the name, and the devilish marquess that wears it all too well, she nearly ends up compromised. Refusing to fall prey to Wesley's skillful seduction, Kate decides to turn things around on the rake. But the high-stakes game between them soon leads to her losing the last thing she expected...her heart

.

BONUS! Chapter One, A Mistress for Penndrake (Entangled Publishing – Amara)

Chelmsford, England, 1814

My dearest Kate,

I have made a grave mistake. Please forgive me. In my absence, promise me you will not engage in any way with a man by the name of Lord Wesley. If he befriends you, walk, and if you are able, run away.

Yours,

Edward Garrett

Miss Kate Holden frowned at her cousin's letter, wondering if he'd been bitten by a terrifying insect in India and since developed a delusional fever. For one, Kate didn't know anyone by the name of Lord Wesley, and even if she did, she doubted he'd ever take the time to introduce himself. After all, what would a titled gentleman want with a tradesman's daughter?

Deciding that Edward had sent the letter in error, Kate smiled and snapped the white sheet into the crisp air, watching it float like a feather onto the high green grass at her feet. Although brisk, the early autumn air was a welcome change from Camden Hall, her home for the last six months.

It had been her dear mother's idea for Kate to visit her wealthier relations so that she may find a gentleman relatively single enough to marry. It was also anticipated Kate was to help propel her cousin, and Edward's eldest sister, Miss Claire Garrett, into the marriage market.

"Marriage," Kate scoffed, having avoided the entire ceremony since her fifteenth year, when a young man stole her besotted heart, and then right in front of her, trampled on it with his foppish slippers. Since then, Kate was glad she had seen the ways of cowardly and despicable men. It helped her prepare for the rest of her life without one. First, however, she needed to help her aunt find companions for her daughters, an endeavor that had proven much more difficult than anyone anticipated.

It wasn't as if Claire lacked beauty or accomplishments. The eldest Garrett sister was much like her younger sisters,

Deidra and Lilly, whose skills were developed and perfected for the sole purpose of luring in dutiful husbands. Deidra played the harp like an angel. Lilly spoke fluent French, and Claire, well, Claire could flirt her way out of Traitor's Gate.

To everyone's disappointment, however, the season had turned into an enormous failure. It not only left Kate's aunt and uncle dumbfounded but the whole town a den of gossip and speculation. Therefore, Kate stayed on, consoling the Garretts, all the while shaking her head at the way women paraded themselves before rows of lying and dishonorable young men for false security.

With her own eyes, she'd witnessed the consequences of at least two young women who'd lost favor with society for their trust and naivety. Shunned by their friends and family, they lived outside of London, destined to die alone and impoverished. *Oh, what a suffocating death.*

If only they had learned more than Latin or how to play an instrument, they might have stood a chance of making a decent living.

Kate chewed on her bottom lip, struck by her own lack of

skill in anything but language and piano, an instrument she played quite poorly. She wondered if it might do her well to explore an occupation that did not cater to the upper class. But what? With her stay at Camden, she'd only learned to mend, to fetch, and to tighten. Why, she'd even developed the useless skill of repairing a table leg after Claire's temper got the best of her one evening.

Her long sigh carried with the breeze. Above all, she supposed her most invaluable lesson came from Mr. Arthur Rourke, who had taught her about a man's affection early. She harrumphed. Was it a habit of handsome gentlemen to shower their beloved with devoted affection one minute, then introduce their most unfortunate beloved to their young bride the next?

To say love had devastated her at such a young age was an understatement. It was as if she'd rushed toward it, tripped, and fallen into a narrow abyss of heartache and tears. She'd landed hard, almost suffocating from the impact, never wanting to experience such an unendurable pain again.

"Good riddance," she mumbled, as bound and determined as ever to remain faithful to her independent and unrestricted spinsterhood. She'd even written to a few families in the south of

England to see about a governess position.

She hadn't chosen this path easily, but she needed to make a living to support herself somehow. There, of course, was an obstacle to Kate's attempt at remaining devotionally single for the rest of her life, and that was her parents' campaign to marry her off to her father's apprentice, Mr. David Leisure.

She scoffed, swiping at the loose tendrils falling into her eyes. Not that she was vain, but Mr. Leisure did not suit her in the least. Tall and distracting with a crooked nose, black eyes, and a sniveling laugh, Kate loathed the idea of even spending an afternoon of tea with him. She believed the only thing worse than getting one's heart broken into a million jagged pieces was entering a loveless marriage where the heart lay untouched and cold.

The circle of thought brought Kate right back to Edward's letter. Still befuddled over what it meant, she brought up the letter to read again as she untied the ribbons of her navy blue bonnet.

Lost in her cousin's warning, she neglected her cap until a whispering wind whipped at the sides and threatened to steal it away. She grasped at the tiny strings, but it was too late. Across the green meadow, it tumbled and skipped without a care.

She glared at it for several moments until it blew against a dogwood tree and rested fifty or so feet away. Resigned to go after it, she stood and lifted the hem of her worn gray dress and strode to the mound of roots, planted her feet, and bent down. She wrapped her fingers around the flapping cords, only to have a powerful gust take it from her once again.

"Come back here," she warned, acutely aware she was barking orders to a silly hat. She didn't care. She'd already wasted too much time reminiscing over her brooding heart and Edward's ridiculous warning.

"I mean it!" she yelled across the mocking field as her hat continued its journey away from her.

"Who are you talking to?"

Kate snapped her head up to find a man on a glistening black horse, his stocky figure blocking most of the sun. She lifted her hand to shield the glare and squinted at him. "My hat, sir."

He bobbed his head. "Well, it doesn't appear to be listening."

His voice caressed her for a moment before she dropped

her arm and turned to see her bonnet even farther away, tangled in a briar patch and struggling with all its might to get free.

"Oh bother," she grumbled, picking up her hem to tramp across the high grass in order to wrestle the darn thing from the razor-sharp thorns before evening. She'd only wanted some peace and quiet from her aunt's constant prattling and Claire's endless requests of "Kate, fetch me some tea. Kate, read me a story. Kate, tell Deidra to stop snorting."

In a way, Kate felt sorry for Claire. As young children, they played well together. Claire was sincere and thoughtful. As they grew older, Kate believed Lady Sophia had put so much pressure on her eldest to marry, and marry well, that Claire had turned into a cornered lioness. Kate feared, one day, Claire would seize the first opportunity to free herself and shock everyone, especially her poor mother.

As Kate walked and muttered to herself, beads of sweat gathered around her temples and slid down between her breasts. The hefty breeze was cool, so she didn't know why her face or other intimate parts of her body felt a bit overheated. Nevertheless, she puffed out frustrated breaths, stretching over the knee-length grass until she reached the expanse of snarled brown vines. She drove her hand deep inside where two long spikes punctured her little and middle fingers. Surprised and angry, she wrenched her arm back to her side.

"You should be more careful."

The familiar, penetrating voice caused Kate to whirl around and find the mysterious rider from earlier. He stood with booted feet upon the soft earth, not a few feet away. Her breath caught as her searching gaze drank in his serious features and confident form. Handsome didn't even begin to describe him. Then again, she didn't know what word did—dashing? Dangerous?

He was tall with black hair, the same color as his horse. The shade of his eyes reminded her of the earth—green mingled with brown and blue in a mesmerizing kaleidoscope of colors. His nose was straight, his lips sensual…and twisted into a humored grin. Did he think her predicament amusing?

Adorned in unpretentious clothing—gray breeches, white shirt, white cravat, and a dark-blue tailcoat—she believed him to be no more than a local gentleman out for a ride.

175

He stepped forward, halted, and then nodded toward her hands. "You do realize you're bleeding?"

She shook out of her trance and glanced down to find splotches of crimson dotting her drab day dress. To her mother's chagrin and her aunt's delight, Kate adorned herself in the most unflattering colors to discourage men like the Mr. Rourkes or the Mr. Leisures of her small world from giving her a second glance.

"May I?"

Uncertain of who this man was or where he'd come from, she took a step back. At some point, he should introduce himself. As well, at some point, their meeting had become strange and untoward. Whether or not he thought the same thing, the man smiled and inched closer. When Kate inhaled, she smelled the soap and woodsy scent of him lifting on the now mellow breeze. She stole a glance at his eyes again. They locked her in place. Slow and meticulous, his large hand reached out and enfolded hers. She held back a ripple of excitement at his warm and calloused touch.

"Do you live near here?" he asked, pulling a handkerchief from inside his waistcoat.

Unsure if she should even engage in conversation with him like this, she said nothing, nodding at first, pausing, and then shaking her head. They had conversed unchaperoned for much too long.

He graced her with a crooked smile. "Yes, you don't live near here?"

His enthralling form and the jesting in his baritone voice left her flustered, curious, and entranced. Never had she met anyone so certain of his words or his actions. Not once did he hesitate to touch her or talk to her as if they were engaged or had known each other their entire lives.

She cleared her throat and tried to smile. "No, I've just come from Camden Hall," she said in a whisper and glanced around to make sure there wasn't someone lurking in the wood line. The last thing she wanted was to bind herself to a man, and even worse, a stranger who had not one clue on the rules of proper engagement with a female. Of course, she seemed to have forgotten the etiquette while in the presence of the opposite sex as well. Either she was under some sort of spell or this was a dream.

Undaunted by her thoughts, his palm cradled her knuckles

as his other hand encircled her tiny finger. She thought it excessive for a small cut. However, she remained silent and curious about his presence and his care.

"I'm afraid I'm not very familiar with the place or its residents." His gaze shifted toward the ground, and he paused before adding, "I suppose if I traveled less, I might know more of who they were."

"Yes, sir," she said, giving him a cautious smile. Perhaps this was some sort of dream where the formalities between an unmarried man and woman were not so strict or tedious.

"I am the Marquess of Wesley, Earl of Chelmsford."

A whimper tore from her throat at the mention of his title and name. A gust of wind stole her mumbled words of disbelief, and she staggered a step away from him. He tried to clasp her hand, but she withdrew from his touch.

"You are Lord…Lord Wesley," she repeated, stunned. This was the very man her cousin had warned her about in the letter. The dream she thought she was having had suddenly turned into a nightmare.

He nodded. "Yes." His eyebrows furrowed above his

darkening eyes.

Walk, no, run! Only she couldn't do anything but stand and stare at him. He stepped closer, his intimidating form blocking the sun and turning the air crisper. She stumbled farther back, her hands outstretched to stop him.

"Are you…unwell?" he asked.

"I'm…I'm not sure if us being alone like this is at all…appropriate."

He chuckled before sobering. "And you've just now thought of this, Miss—"

Oh, now he is all about formality.

Braver than she felt, Kate managed to put three feet between them, wanting to keep her name a secret in the formidable man's presence. She had to escape. But since she'd never been blessed with any amount of gracefulness, her heel found the slippery slope of a moss-covered rock. She tried to catch her balance. Only instinct and years of practice caused her to reach out for whatever stood closest, that being the Marquess of Wesley, Earl of Chelmsford.

In desperation, she caught his memorable and capable

hand as it wrapped around her petite fingers. She realized her blunder and strove to unravel herself from his grasp, but his hold tightened. Her inability to right the wrong accentuated her talent for clumsiness, and also managed to drag him down, right along with her.

She squeezed her eyes shut and waited for her bottom to hit the soggy ground. Somewhere between that moment and the next, his muscular arms wrapped around her, their bodies twisting so she landed on him, instead of the other way around.

She smacked hard against his chest, knocking the air right out of her lungs. She tried to catch her breath, her mind jumbled and dizzy and her heart rapping furious against her rib cage.

"A simple no would have sufficed," he said in a lazy, sarcastic tone. She lay gasping, too overwrought to project a coherent word of any kind. He then chuckled, his whole body shaking underneath her.

She struggled to separate herself from him until she realized his powerful arms held her captive. She was trapped like her bonnet in the thickets of the jumbled brambles. Panic sank into her bones as his powerful fingers dug into the thin fabric of her sleeves and pressed her closer to him. The hardness of his muscles and the spicy warmth of his skin entranced her for a second. She lay still, with her heart pounding like the hooves of a hundred thundering horses. She needed to move, to get away. But the strength of his hands around her upper arms gave her little reason to believe she was going anywhere.

Wake up. Wake up.

She screamed the words in her mind, desperate to not know the extent of her cousin's warning. She didn't wake up, and the havoc this man's contoured body was having on her indulgent and curious female senses was much more treacherous than any warning she read from her cousin.

With her limbs shaking, she managed a steady exhale. "You will release me at once, my lord."

He laughed this time, so easy and sure of himself. If Lord Wesley had a trivial amount of honor, she didn't see it anywhere reflected in his kaleidoscope eyes.

"I will release you when you give me your name."

"This, my lord, is bribery and most unbecoming of someone of your rank."

His lips turned down into a straight line. Her hair, once secured into a pair of gold combs, tumbled out and cascaded down onto his wide shoulders. The brilliance of his face in the sunlight became dark and menacing in the shade of her locks.

An uncertain fear should have made her struggle. It didn't. Instead, she lay on him, the heat of his body seeping through her threadbare dress, producing enough heat to ignite a tinder into a flame.

At last, she tried to squirm, her midsection stroking the pulsing rise between his hips. She continued, unaware of what was happening until he growled deep and pulled her so close to his face, she felt the hot tinge of his breath against her cheek.

She held the air in her lungs and closed her eyes, his curved lips a splinter away from touching hers.

"My intent is not to ravish you, but if you move another inch, I swear I cannot promise it won't happen."

Upon his command, she froze. After a long moment of grave uncertainty, she whispered, "Then, what am I supposed to do?"

A wild heartbeat later, his arms fell away. Yanked to her

senses, she clambered onto her side before rising to stand in a position she'd often seen her brothers, Francis and Joseph, use when imitating the infamous boxer "Gentleman" John Jackson.

She supposed she didn't appear near as intimidating, as she elicited an enthralling laugh from her titled opponent. Insulted, she crossed her arms and waited for him to push himself up. He took his time, stopping to place his large, tanned hands upon his bent knees.

He closed his eyes, his thick lashes pulling together in a quick grimace. After a grunting moment, he straightened and turned his full attention to her. In silence, they stared at each other, his irises shimmering more gold than green in the sunlight.

Above them, a swallow twittered a furious song, lasting close to a half minute before Lord Wesley threw his hand out and said, "I demand you give me your name."

Affronted by his lack of civility, Kate bristled and dropped her fists to her side, bellowing back, "You can demand until you are blue in the face, my lord. I will not only refrain from giving you my name, but also insist that you allow me to leave without you following."

She knew she teetered on insolence and impropriety. However, if her cousin had warned her against this man, she didn't have any reason to care about both.

After a few charged moments, he stepped sideways and lifted his hand, giving her permission to pass. She walked, her knees wobbling, back to the sheet and the now infamous letter from her cousin. As her body tingled with the sense of being watched, she dared not turn or think more of the meaning of Edward's letter. Despite his warning, she did not run away from Lord Wesley but instead found herself drawn to him…in the most wicked ways.

Lord Bachelor (Contemporary Romance)

In accordance with his father's will, Edmund has until he turns twenty-six to find a wealthy bride or lose his vast inheritance. To retain his selfish lifestyle, he agrees to join an American dating game show to find the woman who can save him. He doesn't bargain on meeting Abby Forester, an impoverished, spirited American woman who is content to live out her father's dreams in his vintage record shop.

With covert intervention from an unlikely source, Abby lands on the dating game show as one of Edmund's potential brides. As their worlds entangle and love begins to bloom, Abby discovers Edmund cannot marry her and retain his wealth at the same time. Will love keep them together, or will greed triumph and tear them apart?

MINE, FOREVER AND ALWAYS

In Mistletoe (Contemporary Romance)

At twenty-five, Grace Evans is steadily picking up the pieces of everyone else's life. So, when her younger sister decides to turn into a runaway bride just four weeks before the wedding, Grace, drops everything to chase after her and bring her back home. Only, when the trail leads to Mistletoe, Washington, she finds herself at the mercy of the town's most handsome and emotionally unavailable bachelor.

Ex-Army officer, Ayden McCabe, has three creeds in life: never make the first move, never fall in love, and never take anyone to Mistletoe's Christmas Dance. Wanting nothing more than to keep his matchmaking sister from meddling in his personal life, he agrees to help Grace if she agrees to play his girlfriend. Too brunette and meek for his taste, Ayden believes Grace can't tempt him enough to break any of his creeds. He could not be more wrong.

To My Readers

I would like to say thank you for taking the time to read my debut historical romance: *Mine, Forever and Always*. I enjoyed writing Lily and Henry's story so much; they continue to stay with me. I hope you feel the same way.

Join my newsletter at https://www.tammylbailey.com/contact to get upcoming releases, giveaways, and exclusive content.

Thanks so much,

Tammy L. Bailey

About the Author

Tammy L. Bailey writes both historical and contemporary fiction with clever, romantic, and unexpected escapes combining delicious tension and laugh out loud humor.

Before she began writing romance, Tammy served in both the active Army and the Air National Guard. She was once asked if she wanted to become a navigator on a C-130. However, after getting lost to the recruiter's office, she was persuaded to choose another job.

Today, she lives with her husband and two sons in Northeast Ohio where she balances her time between family, her full-time job as a nursing secretary, and being a writer. Whether it's historical or contemporary romance, for her, there must always be a happy ending.

If you want to connect with Tammy or want to know when she'll be releasing her next book, please visit her website at https://www.tammylbailey.com and sign up for her newsletter.

She can't wait to hear from you.

To receive news on Tammy's latest releases, sign up for her newsletter at

https://www.tammylbailey.com/contact

Thanks so much for reading Mine, Forever and Always.

Made in the
USA
Monee, IL